Grace tore op
and breathed i

Seagulls cawed, sea lions barked, and the waves lapped up against the pillars of the building, a symphony of soothing sounds. Yet Grace found no comfort in the beauty around her. She could only think about Mike Kingston's searing rejection. Touching her had disgusted him, as it would most Christians. She was bruised goods, forever tainted in the eyes of "good people" for her sinful choice to have her son alone.

Mike could see the innocence in her son, the helpless victim needing a father figure, but he could not understand her mistake. It was too much for Christians. It had been too much for her own parents to accept. Why should she expect anything more from a religious firefighter?

KRISTIN BILLERBECK lives in Northern California with her husband, an engineering director, and their four young children. A marketing director by profession, Kristin now stays home to be with her children and writes for enjoyment.

HEARTSONG PRESENTS

Don't miss out on any of our super romances. Write to us at the following address for information on our newest releases and club membership.

Heartsong Presents Readers' Service
PO Box 721
Uhrichsville, OH 44683

Grace in
Action

Kristin Billerbeck

Heartsong Presents

To Arin, an amazing and godly woman who inspires me daily.

A note from the author:
I love to hear from my readers! You may correspond with me by writing:

Kristin Billerbeck
Author Relations
PO Box 719
Uhrichsville, OH 44683

ISBN 1-58660-471-6

GRACE IN ACTION

© 2001 by Kristin Billerbeck. All rights reserved. Except for use in any review, the reproduction or utilization of this work in whole or in part in any form by any electronic, mechanical, or other means, now known or hereafter invented, is forbidden without the permission of the publisher, Heartsong Presents, PO Box 719, Uhrichsville, Ohio 44683.

All Scripture quotations, unless otherwise indicated, are taken from the HOLY BIBLE, NEW INTERNATIONAL VERSION®. NIV®. Copyright © 1973, 1978, 1984 by the International Bible Society. Used by permission of Zondervan Publishing House. All rights reserved.

All of the characters and events in this book are fictitious. Any resemblance to actual persons, living or dead, or to actual events is purely coincidental.

Cover design by Ron Hall.

PRINTED IN THE U.S.A.

one

"Mom, can we go get the InCharge CD tonight? It's brand-new." Josh Brawlins flashed his irresistible smile, made even more charming by his two missing front teeth.

"Josh, we can't go out tonight. You have homework, and besides, we haven't the money for such things right now." Grace flipped a hamburger, searing it against the pan. "I just started this job. Things will be better when our steady paycheck starts again."

"Aw, Mom!"

"You know, I remember the days when you begged for more Barney videos. They had *those* for free at the library."

"Mo—om!" Josh whined as though he'd never heard anything so ridiculous. "Everyone at school has the new CD. Plee–ase!"

"Why don't you ask someone to borrow it?" Grace forced a smile as she put the finishing touches on their hamburger buns. "Is that enough mustard for you?" She placed the dish on the table in front of her young son, hoping to change the subject. Her son being a pauper among princes infuriated her and only caused her to harbor more resentment toward his father. What kind of man abandoned his boy? Especially Josh, who seemed to radiate joy from his very soul.

"Hamburgers, again?" Josh crinkled his nose.

"Yes, hamburgers, again." Grace wrangled her feet free from the torture of her high heels. Sensing her son's disappointment, she grasped his chin, pulling his dark brown eyes

5

to hers. "Maybe you can ask for the new record at Christmas."

"Mom, records are from the Dark Ages. We have CDs now." He pulled free and grimaced at his dinner.

"Oh, yes, the Dark Ages where I came from. I forgot."

"Mom?" The innocence returned to his voice, crushing the teenager that lurked within his six-year-old body.

"Yes, Josh."

"You know, we have the smallest house in the whole neighborhood. It's not even a real house. It's a guesthouse next to a real house. My friends call our house 'the rental.' "

Grace swallowed hard, slamming her plate on the table. *When did kids get so sophisticated? When did children begin practicing the latest dance steps at five years old? When did they notice and compare everything, including how many bathrooms one had?* Grace pondered the thoughts before answering Josh gently.

"We do live in a rental, Josh. That means we pay money to someone to live in his house. We're very lucky to live in this neighborhood. You're getting the finest education the public system has to offer." She sucked in a deep breath. Most kids in Josh's class had more spending money in their pockets than Grace had for the month.

"Yeah, but why do we live in a rental? Why don't we have a fancy car that smells like new shoes? Or a house with two doors in the front, like everyone else? Colton says it's because we got no daddy here."

"We have no daddy," she corrected. "Josh, sometimes families are just different. Our family is different. We have each other." Grace looked into his sad, brown eyes and tousled his sandy locks.

How long could she keep up this charade of living in the exclusive Los Altos Hills without a penny to her name? She hoped forever. At least until Josh got to college. Humiliating as it might be, she'd gladly be embarrassed every day of her life for Josh to have an education. He might not have the latest sneakers, but he'd leave with the same education. She smiled smugly. A little shame wouldn't hurt Josh—not in the long run, but it pained her now.

Josh fingered his fork until it flopped on the floor with a clang. "Mom, Jackson said my shoes were his brother's. That ain't true, right, Mom?"

Her eyes slammed shut, and she forced the lump in her throat down. She'd never planned to be a single mother. It wasn't right her son had to bear this burden! "Josh, would you please just eat your hamburger?"

"Don't cry, Mom. I'm sorry. I'm sorry, did I say something bad?"

"No, Josh. You didn't say anything bad. It's good you have questions. Always ask questions, Josh. That's how we learn."

"That's what Fireman Mike says too."

Grace choked on her bite of hamburger. It went down like a rock. "I don't want you talking to that man. He's a nut, you understand?"

"Mom, he's not a nut. He's Miss Jensen's boyfriend, you know."

"Josh, where do you hear such things?"

"He comes to the school all the time, and Miss Jensen gets all funny around him." Josh covered his broken smile, giggling until he had to shove his hamburger back into his mouth.

"I don't want you talking to him, even when Miss Jensen is around."

"You just don't like him 'cuz he goes to church," Josh spat.

"I don't want him filling your head with stories. That's why I don't like him."

"He says Jesus is real, Mom. He told me—"

"I don't want to hear what he told you. God never helped us Josh. We've done it all on our own. Don't forget it. If you want to live in a big mansion like Mr. Traps, you work hard in school."

Josh looked to the ceiling. "Naw, I don't want a big house like Mr. Traps. Then you gotta have people cleaning it and stuff. I want a little house, but I want two front doors. Oh, and a big stereo so I can play my InCharge really loud." Josh stood and whirled about as though starring in his own rock video.

"Then we'd best get to your homework. Finish up."

"I wished you liked Fireman Mike, Mom. You should at least meet him. He's really cool. He has this big truck. He said it's midnight blue. I couldn't tell you because I never stayed up that late, but it's dark, all right."

"Clear your plate, okay, Honey? Here's your homework sheet. It's counting—your favorite."

"Mom, Fireman Mike likes cool music too. He—"

"Josh, what is the deal? Why are you so enamored with this fireman?" Grace dropped her hamburger, her appetite now completely gone.

"Because I knew you'd say no on InCharge, and Mike said he'd buy it for me."

Grace's eyes slid shut with a great sigh. "Joshua Blake Brawlins, we do not take charity. We are not destitute."

"It's not that, Mom. It's a present. He's bringing it over tonight."

"What? Joshua, get in your room. You know better than to give our address to strangers."

"Mo–om! He'll be here any minute. After dinner, he said."

"Get in your room, Josh."

Josh scampered to his room and slammed the door with vengeance. Grace rubbed her throbbing temples. The doorbell rang.

"Who is it?" Grace asked.

"Michael Kingston." He paused. "Fireman Mike."

Grace could hear the smile in his voice, and she mumbled under her breath that Josh was going to pay for this one. Opening the door, she nearly fell backwards at the sight. A wall of a man filled her doorway. Well over six feet, he looked like a weightlifter. *One of those men who has more brawn than brains,* she thought wryly. Still, it wasn't the vision she was expecting. She thought all zealots wore short-sleeved, button-up shirts and carried a Bible. Fireman Mike obviously carried something heavier than Bibles.

"Look, I don't know what Josh told you, but—"

The wall raised a solid hand. "He told me he wanted the new InCharge CD, and I got it for him."

"Why?" She eyed him warily.

"Well—" he stammered, holding out the CD.

Grace ignored the gift, crossing her arms. "Because you thought we couldn't afford it?"

"Yes, actually." Mike made no apologies for his appearance at her door. He didn't try to pretend he was here for anything other than charity. For some reason, Grace looked at him with new eyes. Interested eyes. What kind of single man concerned himself with a poor kid? It wasn't natural.

"Maybe I don't want my son listening to that garbage. Did you think of that?"

He listened intently, but apparently didn't buy her story. "I grew up without a father. My mother didn't have the money for—well, for extras." Mike's blue eyes clouded. "I thought maybe I could help. I don't want anything in return. I promise."

He thrust the CD toward her again. "You can throw it away if you want, but I promised Josh, and I wanted to fulfill my promise."

Grace looked to the floor. Calculations tumbled through her head. How could she afford something like this for Josh? Oh sure, he didn't need it, but Grace knew its importance to her son. She knew this CD was just one more dividing line between her son and the other children. Another stamp, *the poor kid*, across his forehead.

"I can afford five dollars a week. I would have it paid off in a month."

"I don't want your money, Mrs. Brawlins. I want Josh to be happy. This is not like everything else on the playground, Mrs. Brawlins. Music speaks to Josh, and I really felt the desire to get it for him."

"He doesn't need this, you know."

"Of course, I do. Just like I didn't need the skateboard someone once bought me, but it changed my life."

Grace laughed. "A skateboard changed your life?"

"Not the skateboard. The man who gave it to me."

"Mr. Kingston—"

"Call me Mike."

"Mike, I really do appreciate what you're trying to do, but I don't want you filling Josh's head with fairy tales from church." Grace felt a pang of guilt at the denial of her child-hood faith, but she forced it away. "Josh has had to deal with enough in his short lifetime. I don't want him living with false hope."

"But you do want him living without hope." The wall's deep blue eyes narrowed. He wore a rugged pair of torn Levi's and a stretched, navy T-shirt—or was it midnight blue, like his truck?

"I don't mean you any offense, Mike. But Josh's dad isn't coming to rescue him, and neither is any invisible god, so I'd appreciate it if you left the matter alone."

"I'm sorry about your husband. I really am, and I'm not trying to be anything more than a friend to Josh." Mike looked her straight in the eye. "People will always let us down, but God won't. I believe that with my whole heart, Mrs. Brawlins, because I've seen it with my own two eyes."

This guy just didn't give up. *Enough with the heavenly realms already.* Sometimes she wished she'd never heard about the Bible. Right now, she wished she could childishly cover her ears and remove all of the doubt. This was how she was raising Josh, not under harsh law or a bunch of rules, but with love and encouragement. Why couldn't people understand it was her choice? Maybe part of it had to do with the fact that it was the opposite choice her mother would have made, but she wouldn't think about that now.

"It's Miss Brawlins, not Missus. It never was Missus. Does that shock you?" She eyed him harshly, seeing if her words sent his morally upright body to trembling, but he remained steadfast.

"I'm sorry, I didn't know, Miss Brawlins. I'll remember that."

Grace clenched her teeth. For some reason, it bothered her he wasn't annoyed. "Josh is very vulnerable right now. I'd really appreciate it if you didn't fill his head with your beliefs. He doesn't have a man in his life, and he really respects what you say—"

"Maybe there's a reason for that." Josh splayed his fingers across the doorjamb.

She looked into the sincere blue eyes, the strong facial features were enough to weaken her resolve, but she held firm.

"I'm raising my son on solid ground."

"You're raising him on sand."

"What?" Grace questioned.

"Nothing, Miss Brawlins. You're right. Josh is your son, and it's your business to guide him." He held out the CD again, and Grace ignored it. "I can't help but feel a kinship to him. He reminds me so much of myself as a young boy. I don't want anything from you or Josh. I just want him to know I'm here if he needs someone."

"*I'm* here, Mr. Kingston. He's my responsibility." Grace began to close the door.

"Wait!" He stuck the CD through the crack. "It's not like I'm buying you groceries, Miss Brawlins. Please don't be so proud. It's just a CD. It doesn't mean anything. I know my mom wouldn't have had the money for it. That's all. Besides, every other kid at Los Altos Elementary had it yesterday. I just want Josh to feel he belongs."

Grace opened the door a little wider and blinked her tears away. "Thank you," she managed. She grasped the CD and looked into the wall's brilliant blue eyes. They were the color of exquisite cornflower sapphires. She didn't see pity, or even pride, in his gaze, simply concern. Mike turned and headed toward his truck, and with a roar of the engine, he was gone. Grace's heart pounded, and she wondered at her feelings. Why should it bother her that a total stranger just drove off?

Josh came running toward her, a bundle of energy. "Is that it? Is that it? Give it to me!"

"Joshua Brawlins, where are your manners?" Grace held the gift high above her head. "Now, since I have your attention, this CD is available to you when your homework is finished each evening. It doesn't go on until you've finished. Do you understand?"

"Yeah, Mom!" Josh jumped up and down, trying to reach the coveted music. "I told you Fireman Mike was cool."

"Yes, you did." Grace had to agree, handing him the present. Josh was off like a skittering squirrel. Mike Kingston was definitely cool. The question was, how big a threat was he to their way of life?

She sighed aloud. It would do her no good to fight the virtuous fireman. Josh thought highly of the guy, and as long as he was supervised when with him, what harm could he do?

&

"Well, she let him take it." Mike settled into the driver's seat and looked to Emily Jensen, his girlfriend of two months, and Josh's teacher. "I'm glad she let him take it. I wish I could let her know that I really don't want anything from her. She appeared a bit suspicious."

"I think it's great what you're doing, Mike. She *ought* to appreciate it. I mean, why wouldn't she?" Emily's voice carried a tinge of disapproval.

"Because she's been taught she has to do everything on her own, that's why. You have no idea what it did to my mom." Mike shook his head, remembering. "Miss Brawlins was never married to Josh's dad, and who knows if she's ever been able to trust anyone." Mike watched the quiet little house with melancholy.

"Great. Another out-of-wedlock mom—just what I need to deal with in the classroom every day. Single moms aren't doing me any favors as a teacher. Is it too much to ask that people get married before they bear children?"

Mike let out a short laugh. "It might help to remember behind every single mother is a father who didn't do his part."

"Women get themselves into those situations, Mike."

"I'm sure Josh's mom would have taken your opinion into

consideration if she knew she was going to be abandoned." Mike tried to keep the anger from his voice. "We all make mistakes, Emily."

It was so easy to judge, so easy to stand outside and blame—but he'd been there. As if it were yesterday, he remembered his mother clinging to his father as the burly man tried to shake her from his large frame. The last picture he'd ever have of his father. And the echo. The fury of the slamming door as his mother sobbed.

Emily frowned. "Mike, I didn't mean—"

"Let's just drop it."

"I only meant I've dealt with Miss Brawlins. She's not exactly the warmest woman in the world. I can't imagine her appreciating much of anything, much less a favor from a stranger. I just think your charity might be better spent elsewhere."

"It's not about if she appreciates me, Emily. It's about Josh. The boy doesn't know how to play football, basketball, or even soccer. All the kids at school are friends from outside activities and play dates. Tell me how the kid is supposed to make any friends or be successful if he doesn't have the simple boyhood pleasure of sports or an invitation to any parties." Mike shook his head.

Emily stared at him, her mouth agape. She snapped it shut. "I don't know, but quite frankly, I don't think it concerns you. Lots of boys don't play sports." Emily shrugged. "I don't mean to sound coldhearted, but just because you grew up without a father, it doesn't mean you're responsible for every fatherless boy out there."

"It's different with Josh." Mike wondered at his own words. Why was it different for Josh? Probably, because Mike couldn't erase the boy's image from his mind. Josh was everything Mike had once been: tentative, clumsy, and starving for a father figure and male attention. Mike couldn't explain his feelings or motives, but he needed to be there for Josh. He felt it as intensely as he'd ever felt anything.

"Mike, they have programs for kids like Josh—after-school basketball leagues, Big Brothers, lots of things. I think you're taking this too personally. You have enough worries at the firehouse. Risking your life everyday is not exactly a stress-free lifestyle. No one expects a single man to take on this role." Emily smiled at him, placing her hand on his.

Mike shook his head. "God does, or He wouldn't have sent me the heart I have for Josh. It's really easy for us to ignore the needs we see around us, Emily, but I don't think I can just let this one go."

Emily pulled her hand away abruptly and tightened her arms around her chest. "She'll just sue you for something ridiculous." She turned to stare out at the dark night. "I think it's great you bought Josh the CD, but leave the rest to God and to Josh's mother."

There was nothing hard-hearted or mean-spirited about Emily. She just obviously didn't agree with Mike's latest ministry.

Mike unconsciously clenched his jaw. "That's the way Christians seem to operate in this town. No one looks after anyone else, or cares." Mumbling to himself more than speaking aloud, he softened his tone. "Church is just a consumer product where you pick the best programs rather than a heart for the Lord. Well, I expect more. Jesus expects more."

two

Grace tucked Josh into bed, kissing his warm, round cheek. He was still a baby. *Her baby.* Josh still giggled at childish cartoons, built towers with blocks when he thought no one was watching, and made car noises with his Hot Wheels on the bathtub ledge. Yet, he also studied the InCharge videos that came on during cartoon commercials and practiced the dance moves in the mirror. When had *image* become a part of his little life?

She shook her head and wiped away her tears, wishing she could hold him back. "You are so cool, Josh. If you only saw yourself as I see you. You wouldn't have to prove a thing." She rubbed her sleeping child's forehead. "Your father missed the best thing he could have ever been a part of." *Probably the only thing he ever did right,* she added silently.

The telephone broke her reverie, and she pulled it off the hook before it woke Josh. "Hello."

"Gracie?"

"Lyle?" Grace's stomach turned, and she fell against the kitchen wall at the sound of her past. "How did you get this number?"

"I heard you were working for Holmby and Falk. I got your number from one of the secretaries."

Grace tried to still her trembling hands. "If you'd called my lawyer, I'm sure he could have helped you." She lowered her voice. "Does this mean you plan to help support your son?" Grace's heart pounded like a steel pole driver.

She heard Lyle take in a deep breath of air and give an exasperated sigh into the phone. "This again? After six years, that's all you have to say to me? Listen Gracie, I didn't call about that illegitimate kid of yours. I thought we had that squared away. I'm back in town, and I thought—"

Grace had to keep herself from becoming sick. One night. If she could take back one night in her life. *No.* She forced away the thought, shaking her head unconsciously. *Then there would be no Josh without that one night.* For all her mistakes, all her sins, she was still blessed. Allowed to be called a mother when she deserved nothing so gracious.

She'd known better. Raised in a Christian home, she'd been taught right, but this man. . .this charming snake of a man said so many beautiful words. He wrapped around her with his pretty talk until she became constricted. How could she know he would bite her like a cobra, draining her of romantic emotions for good?

"I don't want to hear what you thought, Lyle. I'm not quite so naïve anymore. I'm not interested in seeing you. Ever. Unless you're ready to talk about financially contributing to your son's education."

"It's no use holding a grudge, Gracie. We were younger, more passionate. I guess I got carried away thinking about the past, coming back here. I transferred from the Chicago office. If you don't want to see me, you don't want to see me, but let's not start this again."

"The only thing I want to see from you is money for our son." She heard Lyle talking to someone in business tone, and her hands began to sweat. "You don't even have to see us. You can simply deposit it in an account for his college." She tried to keep the desperation from her voice. "I think I've been more than fair."

"Unless you have DNA evidence that kid is mine, you'll never see a dime from me. It was a mistake to call. You're still as whiny as ever." The phone slammed in her ear.

She looked at the handset for a moment and placed it back in the cradle. "It's your loss, Lyle. I'll raise this fine boy and work three jobs if I have to, just to prove you had nothing to do with his greatness." She would never submit Josh to a demeaning test to prove that snake was his father. They were better off alone.

"Mom?" Josh rubbed his brown eyes, squinting to avoid the kitchen light. "Who was that?"

"It was no one, and I mean that from the bottom of my heart." Grace grimaced and took her son into an embrace, squeezing as tight as she could.

"Mom, you're smooshing me."

"That's because you are the most smooshable, loveable, gorgeous little kid any mother has a right to call her son." She loved moments like this, when Josh would let her baby him just a little bit. The stress of the phone call evaporated in her son's hug.

"I'm sorry about the CD, Mom."

"I know." She nodded.

"I have an idea for us," he said brightly. "I want to talk it over with you."

Grace glanced at the clock. "It's a little late for discussions, Josh. Can we talk about it in the morning?"

"Well, yeah, but. . .I just wanted you to know I think you should marry Fireman Mike. He'd make a way cool dad, and then we wouldn't have to live in the rental."

Grace laughed, thinking a fireman's salary was probably not much better than hers. "I bet he would make a cool dad, Josh. But don't you think Miss Jensen might have something to say about that?"

Josh shrugged. "She can find a new boyfriend."

Grace lifted her eyebrows. "But I can't?"

Josh crossed his arms. "You'd probably pick some doofus who wore a business suit and walked around with a cell phone in his ear. Like the kids at school. Their dads. I don't want *that* kind of dad." Josh wrinkled his face in disgust. "Yuck."

Grace had to snicker. That's exactly who she had picked, and look how it turned out. Too bad she didn't have Josh's discernment when she was twenty-one years old.

"So Josh—if I can't get you Fireman Mike as a dad, what is it about him you like?" Grace crossed her arms. "You know, just for reference sake."

"Well." He bit his lip, bringing a finger to his mouth. "He has to be strong so we can play sports, and the other kids gotta want him as a dad so they can be jealous."

"Anything else?"

"He should like cool music and drive a cool car. Not one of those fancy SUVs with the classical music and news blaring. A real car, like a truck."

Grace nodded. "Okay, I think I got it. Cool, muscular, and with a truck. Now get to bed. It's nine o'clock."

"Really, Mom, I'm serious."

Grace bent down, looking her son directly in his bright eyes. "Son, there's a good chance we might never have a dad in our house. We have to make the best of it, okay?" There was a very good chance, for Grace would never trust herself to select a man. Clearly, it was a skill that eluded her.

Josh nodded, looking resigned. "Night, Mom."

"Good night, Sweetheart. I'm sorry the phone woke you."

"That's okay, Mom. You're the bestest ever." Josh kissed her on the cheek and scrambled back to bed.

The phone rang again, and Grace reluctantly answered it. "Hello." She swallowed hard waiting for the voice to respond. Knowing it might be *him* again.

"Miss Brawlins?" A low voice with a hint of friendliness replied, and Grace released her breath.

"Fireman Mike?"

"Yes. Listen, Miss Jensen gave me an earful on the way home, and I think I might have made a mistake giving Josh that CD without you knowing about it. I'm really sorry if I offended you. It wasn't my intention."

Grace blinked a few times. Was this a man showing humility? She narrowed her eyes. What could he possibly want from her? She'd never heard a man apologize unless he had an ulterior motive. "Right, well, is that all?" Grace stammered.

"Miss Brawlins, that's all. I just wanted to say I was sorry."

Grace instantly thought of Josh's request for a father, and wondered at the man on the other end of the line. Although he was incredibly large in size with hulking shoulders and massive biceps, she could not believe the gentleness she heard in his voice. He mystified her. She chose to change her tone for Josh's sake. There was no sense pushing away the only man who showed interest in her son.

"We appreciate it, Fireman Mike." Grace paused. "I'm sorry, I don't remember your real name all of a sudden."

He laughed, and she followed suit at her treatment of his name—as if he was a public television character. "It's Mike Kingston. Michael when I'm formal, which I never am."

"Well, Mr. Kingston. You really made Josh's day, and I'll be sure to get you the money as soon as I can."

"Miss Brawlins—"

"We're not destitute, Mr. Kingston. We're not on the welfare rolls yet, and we have a nice roof over our heads so—"

"But there's no money for extras."

"What?"

"There's no money for extras like CDs or designer shoes. Am I right?"

"Mr. Kingston, I don't think that's any of your business. We are not Los Altos's charity case, and we are certainly not yours."

"No, you're not. I work with the charity cases during the Marines' Toys for Tots drive. You have it far better than many."

"What are you trying to say, Mr. Kingston? I'm afraid I don't follow you."

"I like Josh. He's a good kid, and I just wanted to do something nice for him. I'm not trying to make you look bad. I promise."

"Why Josh?" She leaned against the kitchen wall, waiting for his answer.

"Because one day I saw this little boy sitting on the playground alone, and I started talking to him. He told me all about his awesome mom, his love of everything InCharge, and just generally stole my heart. It was like stepping back twenty-five years. He's just the kind of kid you want to be around."

"I agree."

"I'm not trying to take anything from you, Miss Brawlins. I'm just trying to be some type of male role model for your son. I know it's not something you asked for, but can't you appreciate it for Josh's sake? Miss Jensen is always with us. I'm never alone with him, if that's what you're worried about. And Josh likes me. We have some sort of connection."

Grace bit her lips to hold back her cry. She liked him too, as much as it pained her. Any man who saw the special warmth in Josh could not be all bad, and Josh did need a role model.

"Miss Brawlins, you still there?"

"Uh-huh, I'm here." Grace didn't know how to tell him she wanted Josh to spend time with him. The request wouldn't form on her lips.

"Come to church with us on Sunday and see. Josh is interested in things of the Lord. He's a very perceptive child."

The back of Grace's neck bristled. "No. Look, you might be a great role model for my son being a fireman and all, but no religion. Okay?"

"It's not religion, Miss Brawlins. It's faith. Josh asked me about it. I never brought it up."

"Josh asked you about religion?"

"He asked me about God, yes. I told him what the Bible says."

"When did he ask you about God?" Grace had never heard Josh mention any interest in the heavenly realms. The fact that he'd discussed it with a stranger made her heart quicken.

"About two months ago when we met on the playground. He wanted to know if his grandpa was in heaven."

Grace moaned. "His grandpa is in Modesto."

"What?"

"Never mind. Look, I don't mind if you spend time with Josh. I'd actually appreciate it." The words came easy now that she wished to avoid a different topic. "Just no church, okay?"

"Agreed. Can I take you both to dinner Sunday, then?"

Grace's hand flew to her chest. "What?"

"I'd ask Miss Jensen along, but I think being Josh's teacher, she might make him a little uncomfortable. What do you say? Just a simple dinner. . .Chili's?"

Instinctively, Grace smoothed the back of her hair. This was too close to a date for her comfort. "No, no. I don't think so."

"I just want you to be comfortable with me, Miss Brawlins. For Josh's sake?"

Grace shivered. Was there suddenly a chill in the room? "We'll see."

"Ooooh," Fireman Mike clicked his tongue. "I know what that means. When my mom said that, it was a nice way of saying no. Plee—ase—that's what I used to whine to my mom. Of course, I was a lot cuter back then."

I doubt that, Grace thought to herself. "Very well, dinner. For Josh's sake."

"I hope I won't be *that* bad of company. But you can endure me for one meal."

Grace doubted Fireman Mike would be anything other than charming, and that's what scared her silly. "Good night, Mr. Kingston."

"Mike."

"Good night, Mike."

"See you Sunday."

Grace hung up the phone, a wide smile breaking across her face. "Sunday." She sighed.

three

Mike's head jerked up at the sound of the alarm, and his heart pounded against his chest. The adrenaline rush—it was as fresh today as it was ten years ago when he started training. Every time the bell sounded, his heart started that powerful beat, making him feel like Superman himself. Adrenaline was his friend. It fought the fear. It pushed away thoughts of flames and tragedies and allowed him to focus on his mission.

Mike raced to the truck and got in while the crew followed suit. After they drove a block or two, he flipped the switch, and a wail of sirens and lights animated the massive, red engine. He listened to the call on his earphones: Los Altos Elementary. Josh and Miss Jensen's school. He pushed away his fearful thoughts. He muttered his usual prayer, only this one was more insistent.

"Punch it!" Mike yelled, and Kyle did just that.

As the engine pulled in, all the children and teachers were lined up neatly on the grass. He breathed a sigh of relief at the sight. He sniffed the air. It was absent of smoke, and there were no flames in sight. He looked at his partner, Jared, and they nodded in a silent acknowledgement.

As though guided automatically, the firemen searched the school thoroughly. Mike scanned his quarters with a skilled eye and nose and returned to meet his partners. A simple nod from all the men in uniform led their captain to the principal.

"All's clear. You can send the children back in," the captain announced.

The principal motioned to his teachers, and the giggling parade of children started.

Mike's attention rested on the principal, who held Josh by the back of his striped shirt. Josh had great tears rolling down his cheeks, and Mike forced down his own emotions.

"Is there a problem?" Mike asked the principal.

"This is the boy who pulled the fire alarm. He's coming with me, and we're calling his parents." The principal's eyes were narrowed, and his scowl ready. Clearly, this was a man who knew how to intimidate six year olds. "I'm sorry to have caused the department any trouble." He grimaced at an obviously frightened Josh.

Josh looked up at Mike with a pleading expression.

"Would you mind if I had a word with the boy?" Mike asked. "Sometimes the uniform can show the importance of playing pranks."

"Be my guest." The principal released Josh with a slight push.

Mike held Josh's trembling shoulders, and the rush of emotion came pouring out of the child. Racking sobs shook Josh's little frame. "Not yet, Josh. Not yet. You just wait until we're out of earshot, okay?" Mike whispered.

Josh nodded, sniffling.

Mike walked him over to the playground and sat him on a platform. "What's this all about, Partner? You didn't pull that alarm, did you?"

Josh nodded again.

Mike's shoulders slumped. "Josh, you know better. As firemen, we think someone's hurt when we hear an alarm. I've seen a lot of people hurt. It's not something to tease about. Do you understand that?"

Again the little bobbing head agreed.

"So why would you have pulled the alarm?"

Josh looked around him, then finally directly at Mike. "My fifth grade student buddy, John, told me to do it."

"You know better than to do what other kids tell you when it's a bad thing. That's no excuse."

Josh sniffled. "He said he'd beat me up if I was too chicken, and he'd tell his teacher he didn't want to be my buddy in class. He said I was a worm and made fun of my pants. I don't like him." Josh looked to the wood chips that lined the playground. "I told Miss Jensen I didn't want to be his buddy. He's always yelling at me and stuff."

"You know he can't beat you up at school, and now you're going to be in trouble with the principal. Do you see that this was not a smart thing to do?" Mike gently patted Josh's back. "From now on, you tell Miss Jensen if someone threatens you. Don't try and handle it yourself."

Josh shook his head. "He's mean, Fireman Mike. He acts all sugarlike to Miss Jensen. She'll just think I'm a baby too."

"No one thinks you're a baby. Come on, I'll go with you to meet with Mr. Walker."

"Are they going to call my mom?"

"I think so, Sport. It's a pretty serious offense to pull a fire alarm when there's no fire."

"I'm sorry, Fireman Mike. I didn't mean to scare nobody. Are you mad at me too?"

"I'm disappointed you listened to that older kid, but I'm not angry with you, Josh. Let's go see what Mr. Walker has to say." They walked to the office where Mr. Walker worked in his office. The building's brightly decorated walls and modern office equipment belied its tender shape.

Most alarm systems were now equipped with fire alarm annunciators to show if there was a fire and in which zone.

He looked to the wall in disgust. This one had probably been installed when the school was built. Of course, the wealthy parents of Los Altos had provided everything else a private school might acquire. The walls might crumble around them, but they'd be painted in the latest fashionable color.

"Mr. Walker?" Mike stuck his head into the man's office. "Josh Brawlins is here, and he has an apology."

Josh looked up at Mike before speaking. "I'm sorry, Mr. Walker. Someone told me to pull the red handle, and I did it. I knew it was wrong."

Mike nodded proudly at Josh, clutching the little boy's shoulder.

Mr. Walker looked sternly over his glasses. "Well, Son, I've called your mother. She should be here soon."

Mike saw Josh start to shriver again, and he winked. "It's okay, Buddy," he whispered.

"Please don't make my mom come here, Mr. Walker. She just got this new job, and she told me she can't afford to be away from it."

Mr. Walker laughed. "Well, that's a new one."

Mike failed to see any humor in the situation and spoke up for Josh. "Josh just has his mother, Mr. Walker. Her job is very important to them."

"Well, then Josh shouldn't pull fire alarms and call the fire department here. Isn't that right?"

Josh nodded. "Yes, Sir."

"As a fireman I must agree, but I also think we need to look at Josh's age and his accomplices."

"Thank you for your help, Mr. . . . ."

"Kingston."

"Yes, well I appreciate your trying to scare our young friend into not doing this again. I'll handle it from here."

Mike nodded, taking one last look at Josh. "Of course, Mr. Walker." He couldn't resist a final blow. "It might be wise to talk to the district and update that alarm system. If there were a real fire, we would have had to sniff it out. Antiquated systems can harm children."

"Yes, well, thank you. I'll be sure to speak to the taxpayers about it."

Mike shook his head. "See ya, Josh. You hang tough." Mike offered a thumbs-up sign as he exited.

His fellow crew waited in place with all their earphones and equipment ready for departure. Mike quickened his step when he saw Grace Brawlins get out of her car. He looked at his engine, then back at her. He held up a finger to the other firemen and jogged toward the young mother.

"Miss Brawlins."

"Oh, Mr. Kingston, is everything okay?" Grace's pretty blue eyes sparkled under the sunlight, and he suddenly forgot the words at his lips. Grace Brawlins was a portrait of beauty. She had a small ruby-colored mouth, a turned-up nose, and the most flawless skin he'd ever seen. His mouth went dry as he scanned her delicate facial features.

"Mike?"

He gulped. "Everything's fine. Apparently, Josh's older buddy at school dared him to do it, so Josh pulled the fire alarm."

Grace's eyes flashed. "What? I told them I wanted him to get a new buddy. That kid was scaring Josh. Is his name John?"

"That's what Josh said. Go easy on him. He's really scared."

"Thank you, Mr. Kingston. But it's not Josh who you need to worry about. It's your girlfriend and Mr. Walker." Grace straightened her shoulders, and her heels clicked in a determined march toward the office.

Mike watched her walk away, mesmerized by her tiny figure and the fierce mother lion who lurked within such a gorgeous package. He shook such thoughts from his head. Proverbs thirty-one described true beauty, and it was not available just on the outside according to God. His crew honked the engine horn and startled Mike back into the moment. He jogged toward the engine.

૨

Grace Brawlins could barely contain her anger. Her teeth threatened to grind themselves away, and she shook so it was hard to stay upright on her weakened legs.

"I'm here to see Mr. Walker," she told the secretary, who scrambled into an office and whispered something. Mr. Walker held her son by the scruff of the neck. "I'd appreciate it if you'd remove your hands from my son."

He did so without hesitation. "Mrs. Brawlins, if you'll please come into my office."

Grace followed the man and grabbed Josh's hand, squeezing it tightly. "Mr. Walker, I'd appreciate it if Josh would be allowed to go back to class. I'd prefer to speak with you alone."

He nodded. "Tell Mrs. Hanson to get you a pass and run back to class."

Josh scrambled like a cat avoiding an oncoming vehicle, and Grace was left alone with Mr. Walker. Small in stature, he wore nearly invisible eyeglasses with almost no frames to hold them in place. He dressed like the wealthy parents his school served: a pressed pair of slacks with a button-up shirt, a tie, and no jacket. Standard for the Silicon Valley.

"Mrs. Brawlins—"

"Miss Brawlins," she corrected.

"Yes, well, Josh hasn't been in my office before today, but I have heard from Miss Jensen that he can be a problem. A bit on the whiny side, wanting to be coddled and the like." He removed his rimless glasses, setting them on his oversized, metal desk. "This is a very serious issue with the fire alarm. It's a five hundred dollar fine and a mandatory day of suspension."

Grace stood, setting her outstretched arm on the desk. "You listen to me, Mr. Walker: I understand about rules, I understand about fines, and I know Josh has some issues, but let me tell you something. I told you a month ago, in writing, that I did not want that child, John Taylor, near my boy. I told you that he was a bully, scaring my son, and introducing him to culture I don't want him knowing about—Japanese cartoons with sexual overtones and more." She drew in a deep breath. "I want my son held accountable for his behavior, but at the same time, I want this school held accountable for its own. You have a responsibility to protect my son, and judging by today, you did not."

He cleared his throat. "Yes, well. John Taylor is from one of the finest families in Los Altos Hills. Clearly, I don't think *he's* the problem. John Taylor did not pull the fire alarm; your son did."

Grace clenched her teeth, speaking through them. "Just because John Taylor's parents donate large sums of money to this school does not make him a good kid, Mr. Walker. I can tell you stories about that boy that would make your hair stand on end." Grace sat back down and held her breath a moment to calm down. "The fact remains, I told you—in writing—to protect my son from that boy, and I don't think you have. This buddy system you've enacted is a bad idea, and if I have to prove it in court, I will."

The mention of court clearly got his attention. Mr. Walker visibly gulped and broke into a smile, "Now, Miss Brawlins, let's not be rash. We both have Josh's best interest at heart."

"I certainly hope so, Mr. Walker. The fine should be paid. I have no objections to that. He broke the law, and there are consequences. Of course, it's not an amount I have handy, but I will do my best to pay it quickly." Grace sat back in her chair crossing her arms. "However, I do not want that boy allowed within twenty-five feet of my son, and I will do whatever it takes to make sure that happens. If it requires a court order, so be it."

"Miss Brawlins, I'd have no problem upholding such an arrangement if I thought it was warranted, but John Taylor is a good student and respected in this school."

"By whom?"

"Pardon me?"

"Who respects this child? Is it his teachers? The kids on the playground? Who?" Grace bent in, anxious to hear any answer. She knew the only people who had any interest in being around this bully were the fundraisers at the school. John's parents' money bought him a lot of leeway.

"Why. . .everyone," he stammered.

"I doubt that, Mr. Walker. Besides, Josh is not a child who dislikes kids easily. It doesn't matter if I'm right or not—it only matters that I've made my demands known. There is nothing I would consider hard about keeping my son away from a fifth grader. They have separate playgrounds, so I think it should be easily managed during school time."

Mr. Walker sighed. "Very well, Miss Brawlins. And consider the fine paid, but the day of suspension will still have to be served."

Grace smiled and shook the man's hand. "Thank you, Mr. Walker. I hope we won't meet again in such a way, but I love my son, and I want him protected at school. That's my highest priority."

"I understand."

And, Grace thought, perhaps he did.

❧

Grace pulled up to their cottage, and Josh leaped out of the car and ran toward the front door. Although still February, an early spring had brought a bounty of wildflowers, and the yard was an exquisite masterpiece of color. She sniffed the lavender and rosemary and immediately forgot the day's troubles.

She opened the door, and Josh scrambled into his room. Grace dropped her bag on the sofa. She'd miss a day of work already, after only one week on the job. She sighed deeply and fell to the couch, kicking off her heels. "What a day."

Josh came to her side, holding out his new CD as a sacrifice. "Here, Mom. I'm really sorry. Are you going to lose your job?"

"Come here." Grace patted the seat next to her. "You go play the CD and enjoy yourself for awhile, okay?"

"But Mom, I pulled the fire alarm. Even Fireman Mike is mad at me."

"He's not mad at you, Sweetheart. We're both disappointed. We know you know better, but even the best of us make mistakes. Go play your CD. You've had a hard day as it is."

"Mom?" Josh's wide brown eyes met hers.

"Yes, Honey."

"I'm scared to go back to school."

Grace tried to hide her concern. "Why?"

"Because John said if I told anyone he told me to pull the fire alarm, he'd have us kicked out of town."

"Josh, we live in America. It's a free country, although you'd never know it with the price of housing." She looked to her confused son. "No one can kick us out of town, Honey." *They can make our lives miserable,* Grace thought, *but they can't kick us out.* "John is not going to be allowed to come near you anymore. I promise."

"Mo–om! What did you do? He's going to kill me now."

"Don't use that word. He's not going to touch you, do you understand?"

"I'm not going back to school!" Josh ran to his bedroom and slammed the door. Grace flinched at the noise.

"Oh, Lord, if you're up there, why must you test us so? Can't you give my kid a break? Or does he have to pay for my sin for the rest of his life too?" Grace pinched the bridge of her nose, hoping to still the stress she harbored beneath the surface. She let out a short laugh. "Now I'm talking to God. Is there anything more absurd?" Pressing her lips together, Grace flicked on the television and immersed herself in a mindless talk show.

The phone rang, and she ignored it, figuring it was a telemarketer. "Trust me, my zip code has nothing to do with my bank account. You've got the wrong number." But her answering machine came on, and a familiar voice left a message.

"Miss Brawlins? It's Mike Kingston. Fireman Mike. Listen, I know Josh has a mandatory day of suspension tomorrow, and I was just wondering if you two would like—"

Grace picked up the phone. "Mike?"

"Hi."

"Isn't it illegal for you to socialize with fire alarm felons?"

Mike laughed. "Listen, I got the impression Josh was a little upset with me today. I'd like to make it up to him."

"Mr. Kingston, I appreciate your interest in my son, but this is really my problem. We'll manage tomorrow."

Mike cleared his throat. "You've got a son who's afraid of his own shadow. He hasn't got many friends, and he hates school. I've been there, and I want to help. Why won't you toss away that pride and let me help Josh?"

Grace bristled at his accurate, yet searing description of her son. "We'll handle it."

"I'm sure you will, but why not see if I can help? Someone who's been there, Miss Brawlins—I'm offering you the voice of experience."

His sincere tone caused Grace to question herself, but for only a moment. "Quite frankly, I don't trust your motives."

"My motives? What do you think they could be? Every day I face tragedy and death on my job. I've learned that the quality of life is not measured by one's bank account or by one's stellar education. Your son is hurting, Grace, and I think I can help. Please let me, if not for Josh's sake, for my own."

Grace swallowed the lump in her throat. Letting this stranger help her meant giving in to her dreams of full independence. It meant showing Lyle, should he come around, that she couldn't in fact, do this alone.

"I—"

Mike cut her off. "I'll pick you both up tomorrow at eight A.M. Dress casually." He hung up, and she stared into the phone in disbelief.

"Allowing a man to walk over me is exactly how I got myself into this mess, Mr. Kingston." But only an insistent tone on the line answered her.

four

"What do you mean, you're spending the day with them?" Emily Jensen blinked rapidly, and her face was contorted in an unnatural shape. Mike had never seen her so upset, and he lifted his eyebrows in surprise.

"Josh is on forced suspension, and I thought I'd use the day to let Miss Brawlins get to know me." He shrugged, not understanding what had gotten Emily so riled.

Emily let out an unnatural, forceful sigh. "Josh Brawlins is on suspension, Mike. He's not supposed to have a day at an amusement park. He is supposed to be at home, thinking about what he did."

"We're not going to any amusement park, and what Josh did was what any six year old would do when threatened by a fifth grader. Miss Brawlins said she made it known she didn't want Josh around that kid."

"Well, guess what, Mike? We have fifth-grade buddies at Los Altos Elementary. It's not the school's fault Josh can't get along with anyone." Emily crossed her arms, and her brows were lowered in a frightful scowl. "I can't separate the child from everyone because he's afraid to look anyone in the eye. If he needs special help, he shouldn't be in my classroom!"

"Emily, you're Josh's teacher. How can you possibly think that about that sweet kid? He's never anything but respectful, and he scrambles to please."

"If that kid is so sweet, tell me why he doesn't have any

35

friends. Did you ever think of that in your quest to make me a villain?"

Mike's hand raked through his hair. "I'm doing no such thing, Emily. You know that in your heart. Josh dresses in everyone's hand-me-downs in a school where being color-coordinated seems to outrank scholarly pursuits." Mike could feel the blood rushing to his face, and he clenched his hands to try and relieve some of his anger. "You are a Christian woman, Emily, and a kindergarten teacher to boot. I don't see how you cannot love that kid. He's just got a charm all his own."

"I love all my kids, I'll have you know." Emily's nostrils flared. "Josh is just different. It has nothing to do with his being poor, and I resent that you would say such a thing to me."

Mike studied Emily's apartment, trying to get his mind away from this all-out battle they were engaged in. Although only a tiny studio for one, the apartment was decorated lavishly. Emily had set a candlelit dinner in the center of the room on a card table covered by a lace tablecloth. Her futon, which served as both her sofa and bed, was off to the side, covered with an elaborate, lavender floral print. The plates and silverware were lined up to Martha Stewart-perfection, and Mike wondered if he would be able to swallow anything past the angry lump in his throat.

"I'm sorry, Emily. I didn't mean to accuse you of anything. I just think Miss Brawlins's suggestion that John Taylor not be allowed around Josh was not asking too much. After all, Grace knows her son better than any of you."

"Grace?" Emily bit her lip. "You're calling this woman, an unmarried, single mother—and a non-Christian, I might add—by her first name? Did you ever stop to think what your witness might be here, Mike? Hanging around with a heathen single mother and her son is just asking for trouble." Emily turned her back on him, taking out something from the oven. Something that smelled burned. She dropped the pan with a clatter. "I thought your faith was stronger than this. You're missionary dating now?"

Mike focused on the charred meat as she removed the foil. What a fitting sight, because it summed up their dating relationship pretty accurately. It was over. Still, he felt the need to defend himself.

"I am a man of prayer, Emily. I listen to God when He speaks, and I feel called to help that boy. I've asked you time and time again to let me bring him along on our outings, and you've repeatedly turned me down. I don't see what choice I have."

"I take care of children all week. The last thing I want to do is go on a date with them." Emily flipped her brown hair back, looking at the blackened meat and bursting into tears. She blinked her large, tear-filled eyes at him, and he embraced her, patting her back.

"God is calling me, Emily." He whispered into her ear. "If you can't cooperate with me now, you won't cooperate with me later. I'm a firefighter, but I'm a missionary first."

She clutched him tightly. "I never said I wouldn't cooperate. I only said I don't think it's appropriate for you to be involved in this ministry. It doesn't look right."

"Maybe not, but there's something about Josh that has grabbed me by the collar and won't let go. I can't ignore that, Emily. I can't."

"Why must you have Miss Brawlins with you? Don't you care what the appearance of that says?"

Mike looked down at Emily's soiled face. Sadly, he thought she cared little of what his being with Grace looked like to the world. She cared about what it looked like to her, his girlfriend.

He supposed he couldn't blame her. Grace Brawlins was an incomparable beauty, but it was only superficial. Skin-deep. Couldn't Emily see Grace didn't possess the inner beauty he coveted in a wife?

He rubbed her cheek. "Of course I care about my witness, but I care about that little boy having a man in his life, and I care that I feel called by God to be that man."

Emily stamped her foot and pulled away. "What happens if Grace, as you call her, meets some guy and tosses you out of Josh's life anyway? What then?"

"Then I suppose God will lead me when the time comes."

Emily growled in frustration. "You might as well go." She shoved the pan against the stovetop with an obnoxious clang. "There's no dinner here, and there's no reason to stay. You've made your choice."

Mike looked at the dinner, then back at her, but she wouldn't face him. "Please, don't take this out on Josh when he comes back to school. I'm not trying to be difficult. I'm only trying to be there for a little boy who needs someone."

Emily turned to him and pointed a manicured finger in his chest. "You just go be the Christian you say you need to be, and leave me out of it. You go take a kid, who is supposed to be on forced suspension, out for a really fun day. I'll be happy to teach the little monster when he comes back to my world with no consequences for his irresponsible behavior."

Mike blinked away his shock. He'd never seen such venom in Emily and could scarcely believe she possessed it. His mother always said he was clueless with women. Judging by Emily's ugliness, he was starting to believe it.

"I'm sorry you feel that way." Mike grabbed his jacket and walked out the door. Emily could be heard banging pots until he shut the door to his truck.

"That was pleasant." He scratched the back of his head, wondering how he might have handled things differently.

As he drove home, he noticed the lights on at the station house and drove in, parking in the employee lot. The crew was all hovered around the exercise equipment, spurring each other on and shouting up a storm about which of them was weakest. Several dumbbells were lined up to prove each individual's manhood. Mike laughed. *If only women were this easy.* With guys, you knew the game, and you competed. With women, you had to second-guess everything that tumbled from your mouth. It was usually too late by then.

"I notice you have this competition when the real winner isn't around to prove himself," Mike quipped, flexing his biceps.

A collective shout of boos and hisses went up, and Mike broke into laughter.

"I think the fact that you had a date, and you're here at eight o'clock proves that theory wrong." Jared looked at his watch and lifted his eyebrows. "Well?"

Mike shrugged. "Another one bites the dust."

Jared placed his arm around Mike, and they walked outside. Being dumped was off-limits for banter. Most of the firehouse was married, and girlfriends and possible wives were treated with the utmost respect. The men had seen far too much loss for anything but a healthy love and admiration for relationship.

"Sorry, Bud." Jared said when they reached the pepper tree customarily used for such private conversations.

Mike shrugged. "It's no big deal." But inside, it felt like one. Mike was thirty-three and facing facts that he might never be married. Maybe God thought of him as a Paul, the kind better off not being married.

"What happened?"

"You know that kid?"

"Josh?"

"Yeah. I'm spending a little too much time with him for Emily's liking."

Jared smiled and raised an eyebrow. "Too much time with Josh or his mother? I saw her yesterday at the school, remember?"

"I haven't spent *any* time with her, yet."

"A fireman knows better than to play with fire."

"You think that's what I'm doing?"

"Don't know, Man." Jared looked him in the eye. "I know you're a man of prayer, so I can only pray you're in His will."

"I don't think Emily has a heart for ministry."

"Maybe Emily doesn't have a heart for *your* ministry. That's something different altogether."

"Wonder if there's a woman out there who does."

"Sure there is, and maybe it's Emily. Your timing might just be off."

Mike nodded. Sure, maybe that was it. His timing was off. He was trying to force something into happening instead of waiting on the Lord.

"Thanks, Jared."

Jared looked away. "This pepper tree just gets bigger and bigger, huh?"

"Yeah." Mike looked up. "I have to run. I'm picking up Grace and Josh in the morning."

"I'll pray for you, Buddy."

"Thanks." Mike got back into his truck and drove off, the roar of his engine offering a comforting arm around him.

❧

Grace looked at her bills and tossed them on the table. How

would she ever cover the five hundred dollar fine? She could barely pay her electric bill. Regardless of what Principal Walker said, she wasn't about to be a charity case. If there was a fine, there was a fine, and it would have to be paid. She made herself a cup of coffee and sat down with the newspaper. Avoidance felt good for the moment.

She lifted the society page and nearly spit out her coffee at a picture of Lyle Covington smiling, gazing lovingly at a beautiful blond. The headline read, "Defense Attorney Lyle Covington to Marry Star Real Estate Agent, Lily Hampton." Grace's breath left her. How dare he! How dare he go on with his life and start another family without paying for the one he already had. And what was that phone call about? A last hurrah? Well, Grace would give him a last hurrah, and it would come in the form of a child support payment.

Grace looked up the number, and dialed her boss, banging the number out with ferocity. "Mr. Falk? It's Grace Brawlins."

"Grace? Is everything all right?"

Grace breathed deeply. "Well, actually, no, Mr. Falk, it's not. I hate to bother you at home, but I have some private business I'd like to discuss with you. On a professional level."

"Go ahead. Janice? Could you shut my door?"

Grace heard the door close at the other end of the phone, and she began. "Mr. Falk, I want you to know that I am committed to my job as a legal assistant. I know I haven't worked for you for all that long, but I'm good at what I do, and I plan to be there a long time."

"Wonderful."

"That being said, I'll be out of the office tomorrow. My son has been suspended for pulling a fire alarm at school."

"Oh dear," the older man said. There wasn't a hint of judgment in his voice. Having raised four children himself, he was probably very familiar with such antics. "I'm sorry, Grace. I realize you are still in the probationary period at Falk and Lawton, but I think I can trust you. If you must take a day off for your son, you must. I'm a pretty good judge of character, and I know you have it."

"Thank you, Sir. The other concern I have is a bit more of a personal nature. I want to hire the firm to represent me in a paternity case."

Mr. Falk did not react, and for that Grace was grateful.

"Josh's father is about to marry. He's never taken responsibility for the child, and I haven't wanted to press it, but Josh deserves to be supported by his father."

"Are you willing to have a DNA test done?"

Grace paused, closing her eyes. "I doubt I have a choice. Mr. Falk, this man is a prominent lawyer. I was young and naïve—not that it excuses my behavior—but now, he is ready to get married and probably start a family of his own. I can't have Josh always being the poor kid, while this man's other children enjoy country club memberships. It's just not right."

Mr. Falk took in a deep breath and boisterously let it out. "What's his name?"

"Lyle Covington."

"The defense lawyer?"

"The same."

"I have to ask this, Grace: Are you sure he's the father?"

"There is absolutely no question. None whatsoever. He is Josh's father." The words tumbled out of her with urgency. She'd never admitted paternity, not even on Josh's birth certificate; but studying her bills, she knew this was the time. Josh had suffered long enough. He wouldn't have to know what the blood test was for, only that he needed to have blood drawn.

"Are you sure this just isn't about revenge as Mr. Covington gets married?" There was gentleness in the question.

"I wouldn't call it revenge, Mr. Falk. It's about justice. He just can't go and start a new family and leave a trail of father-less children. He just can't. He practices law, and he ought to be made to uphold it. He took the bar to do so."

"Very well, Grace. I'll take a deposition as soon as you return to the office."

Grace sat up straight, willing herself to be brave. "I'm hop-ing you'll be able to reduce your fees a tad. Perhaps—"

"Grace, I don't want you to worry about my fees. This is not normally the type of work I do. I know you understand that. But I wish to make a moral statement with this case, and I'm taking it on pro bono."

"No, no. I don't want to ask that."

"You didn't ask. If you're better able to care for your son, you'll make a far better employee, Grace. I have my own self-ish reasons."

Grace thought Mr. Falk was anything but selfish in his undertaking. She'd seen him running his prayer meetings in the morning. Maybe some Christians really did live like good people. Mr. Falk seemed to. Maybe Mike Kingston did as well. She forced the thought from her head. Believing in peo-ple was exactly what put her in this situation. She wouldn't make that mistake again. For Josh's sake.

"Thank you, Mr. Falk. Thank you."

"Wait and see how we do before you thank me, Grace. I'll see you on Thursday."

"Yes, Sir. And if there's anything you need me to do from home. . ."

"Just enjoy your son, and keep him away from the fire alarms," he said jokingly.

"I will, Sir."

"Good-bye, Grace."

Grace hung up the phone and cried at Mr. Falk's kindness. Searching Lyle's eyes in the photo, she shook her head. His fiancée looked like the type who would make Lyle happy. Even in the grainy newspaper shot, Grace could see she wore far too much makeup and was too buxom to be real. Although Miss Hampton's hands weren't shown, Grace had little doubt her nails were red, long, and clawlike.

"I imagine you think you've made quite a catch, Miss Hampton, when in reality, you should run for your life." Grace dropped the paper back to the table and went to check on Josh.

Josh's angelic eyes were closed in sleep, and his lips were curved into a sweet smile. Grace laughed, thinking about the *InCharge songs or cartoon humor he might be dreaming about. Or maybe it was the following day with Fireman Mike that made him grin so big in his sleep.

Grace felt her heart beat at the thought. Something was different about that man. Although he was built like a wall and blessed with those sapphire blue eyes that reached out to people, he dated the mousy, little Miss Jensen. She was a sweet woman, kind in nature, but she was certainly nothing to look at. That fact startled Grace. She hadn't met any men who didn't just want an elegant package, someone to impress the boys at the club. Those blue eyes would turn any woman's attention in a room, so what was Mike Kingston looking for in a wife?

Or did he want a wife? Maybe he was like Lyle had been. Maybe he just wanted a woman for companionship—a woman to be there when it was convenient—certainly not all the time. Grace rubbed Josh's hair and wished with all her heart Lyle's child support would start soon. Embarrassing though it was to bare her soul to Mr. Falk, Josh would hopefully be the better for it.

"It's time we stopped living hand-to-mouth, Josh. You deserve better."

She rose and closed his door behind her, lamenting the empty house and how lonely it felt once Josh was asleep. This should be her time to do as she wished, but there was nothing she wanted to do. She had no hobbies, no great passion in life, so again she flicked on the television and tried not to daydream about a handsome fireman coming to her rescue.

five

Josh chattered away like an eager chipmunk that had too many nuts to carry. Grace listened to the incessant talk until the words were so rushed, they could not be separated to make any sense.

"Josh," Grace finally said. "Please, just eat your breakfast. Fireman Mike will be here soon, I promise."

"This is the best day ever, Mom!" He looked down at his cereal, whirling it around with his spoon. "Sorry. I know I'm supposed to be in trouble." His eyes brightened, and he continued on, "Do you think we could go to the zoo? What about a baseball game? The Giants play today. Or maybe we could ride bikes at the park. Do you think Fireman Mike has a bike? Hey, Mom, what about hiking up to the old farm? Do you think he'd like that? I wonder if he plays football too. He looks like a wrestling star. I wonder if he ever wrestled."

"Josh!" Grace clutched her head. "Give it a rest, Bud." Josh quietly removed his bowl from the table and set it in the sink. When he turned, his disappointed frown crushed Grace. "I'm sorry, Josh. I know you're excited. It's just that Mommy's coffee isn't ready yet, so I'm not awake enough to be excited yet. Give me five minutes, okay?"

He kissed her cheek. "I like you better after your coffee, Mom."

Who doesn't? Brown liquid, rich in scent, filled the pot. She waited alongside the machine, knowing exactly when there was enough for a cup. As if a bell rang, Grace grabbed the pot and filled her cup. She sniffed it, clutching the mug like a long-lost friend. The doorbell rang, and she longingly opened her mouth before setting the cup back on the counter.

"Good timing," Grace quipped.

She opened the door, and although she tried to be mad, there was something about Mike Kingston's face that prevented it. His dark hair was still damp; his face, clean-shaven; and his sapphire eyes, brilliant. Something about him always appeared to be smiling, even when his face was missing a grin.

"Good morning," she offered.

His eyebrows lifted. "Are you ready for our big day?"

"You are far too chipper this morning, Mr. Kingston. I take it you got your coffee."

"Don't drink the stuff."

Grace rolled her eyes. Was there anything this scout did that might be considered habitual? Josh jumped around like a pogo stick and offered a plethora of ideas for the muscular fireman. Mike held up a firm hand, and Josh immediately halted.

Grace crossed her arms in amazement. "I wish I possessed that skill."

"Now, we have a lot to accomplish in one day, Mr. Joshua Brawlins. It is not every day one gets to play hooky from school." Mike looked to her. "With your mother's approval, of course." He winked, and Grace was mesmerized by the action. Bent over Josh, he had both of their full attention. Something about him just commanded it.

"What are we going to do, Mike?" Josh began to jump again.

"Well, first, we are going to the Monterey Bay Aquarium!"

Grace felt her smile leave, and she shook her head. "Josh, go get your coat."

Josh ran toward his bedroom like a rocket, and Grace approached the wall of a man. His expression softened at her advance, and she noticed again how his eyes smiled even when his mouth didn't. She blinked quickly, trying to remember what she was so upset about, and it finally bubbled up.

"Mr. Kingston, I cannot afford the Monterey Bay Aquarium, and I would appreciate it if you'd stick within our budget today. I'm more than happy to have you come along for Josh's sake, but we need to stay reasonable. Josh can't go thinking I have that kind of money to do such things all the time."

He held up tickets. "Free." He shrugged. "I saved somebody's cat, and they bought me a year's subscription to the aquarium. I'm a member. We'll just have to pay for Josh's ticket."

Grace began to protest when she realized he'd given her nothing to work with. Then, she remembered Miss Jensen. "What about your girlfriend? How does she feel about my using her ticket?"

Mike looked to the floor and put the tickets back in his wallet. "I have no girlfriend. Miss Jensen decided she was better off on her own."

Grace bit her lip. "Oh, I'm sorry." Their gazes met in understanding. Two people who felt the pain of being left. "Truly, I am."

He nodded. "Thanks."

"I'm sure you'll meet someone else at church." She smiled, hoping she'd said the right thing.

"I'll wait on God. He knows who's best."

She chose not to comment, and Josh came back into the room with three jackets. "I've got my raincoat, in case it rains, a windbreaker, in case it's windy, and a ski jacket, in case it's cold."

Grace looked out the window. "Josh, it is seventy degrees already. Go put your jackets away."

"But you just told me—"

"I was wrong. Let's go."

Josh dropped the jackets on the couch and scrambled out to Mike's truck. It was a gorgeous deep blue, darker than his eyes and far less sparkly, but it had room for six and a backseat for Josh.

"Let me just get his booster seat," Grace said.

Mike looked at her, then to Josh's small frame and nodded. Although six, Josh was no bigger than the average four year old. She thought holding him back a year in school would make a difference, but he was still one of the smallest in his class. No wonder he seemed to worship this great big man with the gentle eyes.

Grace pulled the booster from her car, and Mike took it from her, setting it in the center of the backseat for Josh. The truck still had that divine new-car smell. Grace had never owned a new car, and there was something so luxurious about sitting in one.

"I like your truck. It's so comfortable." She ran her hand along the smooth leather.

"I bought it in December. Miss Jensen was embarrassed to be seen in my old jalopy." He laughed, but Grace stiffened. Thinking back to Lyle and his perfect car, she knew a decent vehicle had nothing to do with the interior of a man. If Emily had a lick of sense, she wouldn't have let Mike go.

They rode for a long time in silence, except for Josh pointing excitedly at every new sight they passed.

❧

Cannery Row, made famous in Steinbeck's book, was still quaint. Its old sardine canneries were now transformed into gift shops and fine seafood restaurants. The aquarium stood like a mighty fortress on the edge of the Monterey Bay, its gray color blending into the bold colors of the brown craggy rocks and deep blue waters. The air was fresh and whipped around her in gales. The slight scent of seaweed permeated the scene.

Grace took out her wallet, but Mike pushed it away. "I'm buying."

"No," she insisted. "It's enough you drove us here and had a ticket for me. We're not—" Grace cut her speech short when she saw an older woman staring at her. Something about the look in the woman's eye made Grace step back. Mike went forward and paid for Josh's ticket, and Grace looked to the woman expectantly.

"Let him pay, my dear," she whispered. "A man must be allowed to care for a woman. It makes them feel more like a man. It's nice to see chivalry isn't dead, and I'd hang on to him if I were you." She patted her gray hair and trotted off on the arm of a man—a man who'd obviously been her husband for a very long time.

"Grace?" Mike stood at the doorway with Josh, waiting with the door opened. "We're ready."

She nodded. "Of course." She ventured a look back at the married woman and received a wink and a smile.

Wandering through several exhibits, Josh oohed and ahhed over the sea otters, marveled at the diver in the enormous kelp bed tank, and dropped to his knees, stunned by the shark exhibit.

"Look at that big one, Mom! How do they keep them from eating the fish in the tank?"

A volunteer in a red jacket came closer to them. "We keep the inhabitants of the tank slightly overfed. They are usually too full to think about eating their neighbors, but every once in awhile. . .well, a shark is still a shark."

"Cool!" Josh said. "Maybe we'll see him eat one."

The volunteer laughed. "You can come back for their feeding, at three."

"Can we, Mom?"

"I suppose, if we're still here. We wouldn't want to miss that, now would we, Mike?"

"I have something better planned," he said mysteriously. "Something way better."

Josh's eyes grew wide. "What?"

"You'll just have to wait and see. Let's go pet the bat rays." Mike waggled his eyebrows.

The bat ray tank was filled with skimming, black, winged objects which maneuvered eerily, like birds in flight. Joshua reached out his hand, and Grace tried to grab it back when Mike caught her hand and shook his head. He didn't let go immediately, and she looked into his blue eyes. Whatever he saw in her, he didn't want to see, because he pitched her hand like a bad piece of fruit.

She swallowed hard and concentrated on Josh again. He had reached for a bat ray, and crinkled his nose. "Ewww. It's really slimy, Mom. Touch one."

"I don't think so, Josh." She tried to laugh it off, but the lump in her throat would not be swallowed. "Mike, would you keep an eye on Josh for a minute? I'm going to find the restroom."

"Sure." He nodded.

Grace tore open the doors to the outside patio and breathed in the moist sea air. Seagulls cawed, sea lions barked, and the waves lapped up against the pillars of the building, a symphony of soothing sounds. Yet Grace found no comfort in the beauty around her. She could only think about Mike Kingston's searing rejection. Touching her had disgusted him, as it would most Christians. She was bruised goods, forever tainted in the eyes of "good people" for her sinful choice to have her son alone.

Mike could see the innocence in her son, the helpless victim needing a father figure, but he could not understand her mistake. It was too much for Christians. It had been too much for her own parents accept. Why should she expect anything more from a religious firefighter?

She tried to blink away her tears, but they pounded against her cheeks relentlessly, like the waves below. She thought about Lyle and his healthy check. She laughed at her innocence, thinking he meant it for baby clothes. She clasped her eyes avoiding the reminder of what he'd truly meant by giving her the money. To this day, it stabbed her in the heart to think of his intentions.

First her parents, and now Mike—righteous Christians in her life reminded her she would never be good enough, never worthy to start a new life. Christians seemed to be everywhere, surrounding her 'til she thought she might choke on them.

"Grace?" Mike stood behind her, the brightness of the sun lighting him. He gulped at the sight of her, and she whisked away her tears with the back of her hand.

"I came out for air. Where's Josh?"

"He's right there, watching the otters lunch in the little inlet."

Grace scanned the benches and found him joyously watching the animals.

"He's having a good time." Grace grinned at the sight of her carefree son.

"I wish I could say the same for you."

She couldn't find words, so she just looked away, focusing

on the same otter that held her son's rapt attention.

Mike looked out at the horizon. "I wasn't prepared for what I felt back there. I'm sorry."

Grace lifted her eyes to his, amazed he'd understood what had bothered her. "I understand."

"No, I don't think you do."

"You're a saint. A saint must find another saint. It's in that Bible of yours. I know."

"How do you know?"

"I grew up in a Christian home. I know all about your rules."

His shoulders slumped. "I'm sorry no one's ever shown you Christ's love, Grace. It's not about the rules."

Grace laughed. "Apparently, it is. I can name you quite a few people who would be more than happy to tell you how I fail as a saint."

"I'm sorry, Grace. Truthfully, they don't sound like anyone I want to know. Do we have time for one more adventure this afternoon, or have I ruined it?"

"I think we should be heading back. We're still ninety minutes or so from home."

"Ple–ase!" He clasped his hands together against his chiseled chin, and if there were a woman alive who could resist the request, Grace would love to meet her and shake her hand.

"All right. What did you have in mind?"

"How brave are you?"

She crossed her arms. "Not very. I don't rush into burning buildings for a living; I sit in front of a computer. Does that give you an indication?"

"Ah, you'll be a pro. Think how you can impress Josh."

"Impress Josh with what?"

"That's the surprise. Come on, let's move on." He placed

his hand at the small of her back but quickly removed it when she flinched.

❧

They all piled into the truck as if they'd been doing so forever. Josh buckled his seatbelt, and the adults followed suit. The sun along Monterey Bay sparkled like pure gold on the white caps in the water. Sea lions frolicked everywhere along the shore, and an occasional otter would make Josh squeal with excitement.

Five minutes later, they arrived at a public beach, and Grace breathed a sigh of relief. "Shoo." She hopped out of the truck, helping Josh out when her smile abruptly disappeared. Before her were several kayaks on a rack with a red sign reading "KAYAKS FOR RENT." She looked from the waves crashing on the sand, to the little plastic boats, and back at Mike. She simply shook her head.

"Come on; it will be fun." Mike gave her that wide-eyed look again, and she had to admit it was no less charming than the first time.

"Yeah, Mom, cool! Can we?"

"Josh, look at the size of those swells. We have no experience in one of these things, and we're not going to jeopardize our lives for a cheap thrill." She pulled Mike by his elbow. "Mike, I do not appreciate being the bad guy here. I never agreed to let my son ride in a flimsy boat on Monterey Bay. I agreed to take him to an educational museum. I understand your desire to make a man out of him, but I'd like him to live to see his manhood."

"Grace, there's nothing to worry about. We'll be in wetsuits and life jackets. If we tip, we just climb back in. We'll rent a kayak for three and put Josh right in the center, between us. I'll be in the back, and I'll see everything that happens."

He exuded confidence, but Grace had only to look at the surf again to know she was firm. "No."

"Let me take Josh then, in a kayak for two. Grace, he'll have a blast, and I wouldn't let anything happen to either of you."

Grace looked to her son. He'd never had the opportunity to camp or doing anything remotely so rugged. She nibbled at her lip and took in Mike's brawny arms. Surely, he could fish out wispy, little Josh if something happened. But no, what if something did happen?

"Can you swim?" She finally asked.

"Grace." He crossed his arms, showing the full power of his biceps. "I am a firefighter. I rescue people for a living. Of course, I can swim, and under dire circumstances too."

"Will you promise me Josh will be fine?"

"Scout's honor." He lifted three fingers.

"I'm coming too. There's no way you're going out there while I'm powerless on the shore." She could kick herself for giving in, but if Josh was going to stretch his wings, she needed to let him lift off the ground.

Mike smiled with his whole handsome face. "Great!"

Somehow, Grace wouldn't have described what she felt as great. She believed fear was a better term.

six

Mike paid for the kayak, and he looked to Grace, surprised she didn't argue about money. *I guess she figured I could pay for this harebrained scheme.* With narrowed eyes, she watched the whole transaction, as if heading before a firing squad. . .with him as her executioner. She apparently didn't want to pay for the privilege. Mike had to hide his grin. For all her protests, Josh's enthusiasm kept her from voicing her further objections.

As a final insult, the man behind the counter asked for her weight. Mike offered a sheepish smile, but it didn't appear to work. Grace released her wrath. "Is there a reason you need to know my weight?" she finally asked, cocking her head.

"The wetsuits are calibrated by weight, Ma'am. I can guess if you don't want to tell me," the employee said. Mike fought a smile at the suggestion. Certainly, she'd find that no more appealing. Mike wasn't sure what she worried about. She had a wispy figure, like her son, only she was curved in all the right places. He chastised himself for noticing, but he was a single man, and he certainly wasn't blind.

Grace's eyebrows lifted. "I'd rather you not guess."

The man scanned her quickly, anyway. Mike shut his eyes, preparing for an onslaught of words, but the employee had obviously done this before. "Probably an extra-small. Up to 120 pounds?"

Grace broke into a smile. "Well, I'm five-foot eight, so I'm closer to 124."

Mike let out his breath. Fitted properly in their wetsuits, they made their way toward the boat and their lesson. Josh bounced about like an out-of-control rubber ball, and even looked the part in his black neoprene suit.

"Josh." Mike held his small shoulder to plant him steady. Looking into his big brown eyes, Mike knelt down. "I know you're really excited to go on the kayak, but we have to listen to the lesson now. You need to know what to do to help us out and what to do if you get into trouble. This is important, so I want you to act very seriously."

Josh nodded, blinking rapidly. "Okay, Fireman Mike. Will we see a whale? Or sharks?"

Grace's eyes grew large.

"Probably not, Buddy. We're on the bay, not the open ocean. We'll see some sea otters, though. You like them." Mike did not add that sharks teemed below, but the kayak would be on the surface. Sharks had very little interest in people, and most big enough to do any damage would be out in the open waters. Still, it was information he kept close to his breast.

After a lesson, which Grace panted through most of, they carried the three-man kayak down to the shore. Waves nibbled at their feet, and Grace turned around, as if to run before looking at Josh and relenting by showing him how to get into the kayak. Mike couldn't help but admire the love she showed that boy. Her small frame was shivering from fear, but she put Josh's desires before her own. She helped him into the middle station and climbed to the front.

"I guess we're ready," her voice shook.

Mike held the boat at shore while they positioned themselves, then climbed in to the last seat. "Row!"

Frantically the pair, looking like the two stooges themselves, tried to get the kayak straight. Mike had to laugh. He could easily maneuver the vessel on his own, but what would be the fun of that? Grace caught on fairly quickly, and soon they were past the white caps and into the blue swells. As the water got deeper and darker beneath them, he could hear Grace moaning in her terror while Josh shouted an endless chorus of "cool!"

With the two of them rowing in tandem, the boat sliced through the water quickly, and they came to the end of the wharf. "Turn!"

Grace froze at his order and lifted her oar from the water. "Am I okay?" she asked without turning.

"You're fine. We'll go into this inlet and let Josh see the otters feeding."

Grace nodded gently, clearly too nervous to make any rash movement. He chuckled to himself. Once the kayak was in shallow, calm water, her shoulders visibly relaxed, and she turned to face him.

"Are we done now?"

"No way, Mom. This is cool. Did you see those huge sea lions?"

"Oh, I saw them all right—after I smelled them. Ick." Grace turned around and crinkled her nose in the most charming way. "You know, I never thought of a sea lion as threatening, but when they dive in with a great splash, and you don't know where they'll bob up, they might as well be a treacherous sea monster. I'll gladly give them back their turf."

Grace wore one of Mike's old baseball caps to keep the sun from her eyes, and Mike sat mesmerized by the panoramic picture before him. This is how he imagined his life. Out on the open water, adventuring with his family, taking in one of the most picturesque spots God saw fit to create. He took a photograph in his mind, scanning all the details before him.

Grace's profile resembled a classic painting. Her skin, without a hint of make-up bordered on perfection, and her wide gray-blue eyes held all the innocence of a child. With a name like Grace, he wondered what had happened to harden her so. He knew Josh's father had something to do with it, but he didn't dare ask. Had she been loose in younger days? Had an affair with a married man?

He forced such thoughts away. Judgment was exactly why Grace wouldn't speak of faith, or religion as she sharply called it. If she ever cared to tell him, she would. Otherwise, Mike would focus on loving Joshua and Grace for who they were, not only as potential Christians. For then, he was only a clanging gong.

Rubbing the sand from his palm, he placed a hand in the water to clear away the grains. A flash of silver blinded him. He pulled his hand from the bay. The boat rocked, and Grace and Josh screamed. Mike steadied the kayak with his weight and looked to his two frightened passengers.

"What was that?" Grace asked.

Mike laughed out loud. "It was a fish. A really big fish. I guess my dive watch attracted him, and he thought he might lunch on my fingers."

Grace clutched her heart, but soon broke into a giggle. "A fish? Oh, I'm far too jumpy. All those tales of sharks you've been telling Josh have this mom in a panic."

"You're doing wonderfully. I've never seen anyone take to the oars so naturally."

Her expression softened, and she freed her hair from the baseball cap in a glimmer of gold. "Really?"

Mike swallowed hard and looked toward the rocks. "Look at those sea lions over there, Josh." He pointed toward the shore, aware of her steady gaze upon him. Flirting seemed beyond Grace's world. She wasn't flirting with him; she simply engaged people with her presence. *Careful, Buddy*, he reminded himself. Bringing her back into his view, he straightened his shoulders to appear unaffected by her beauty.

He thought of his girlfriend, now his ex-girlfriend. A relationship wasn't based on physical attraction. Perhaps he needed to call Emily tonight. He should at least apologize for his feeble attempts at explaining himself. Perhaps, he hadn't given it enough of a chance.

"Mike, it's getting late. Do you think we should be rowing back about now?" Grace turned her head and faced him. Her cheekbones appeared almost carved into a sweet heart shape, and he cast his gaze away. *Now he was noticing cheekbones?*

"Yes, I suppose we should. We'll get some dinner and drive back. My stomach is a little queasy after that burger for lunch."

"I saw a McDonald's right across the street!" Josh announced.

"Oh, no. When I say we're going out to dinner, Josh, I mean somewhere the meal doesn't come with a toy, okay?"

Grace laughed. "I don't think Josh has been to the kind of restaurant that doesn't serve value meals."

"Tonight, he's going to try seafood."

Josh shook his head violently. "No way! I don't want to eat a slimy fish. I want a hamburger."

"You can have a hamburger after you try some of our fish," Grace chastised. "And I'm getting dinner. I won't hear any arguments."

Mike nodded. "Fair enough. It's too bad I don't have a place to cook, though. I'm quite a fine chef."

"I thought that was a myth about firemen. A wives' tale, you might say."

"You thought wrong. I bet my comrades could out-serve the best of your housewife friends." Mike put his hand on his hip.

"Well, sure, you guys don't have kids at your feet, yelling if the meal takes longer than twelve minutes to prepare." Grace's lips curled into a smile. "Besides, I don't have any housewife friends. There's something about the married types. They don't care for us single types."

"We have a great singles group at our church." Mike offered before remembering her thoughts on church.

Grace's smile disintegrated. "Ah, you forget I wear a brand." She nodded toward Josh. Deciding it was a conversation best left unstated, Mike turned the kayak around and headed back toward the shore.

Once in the vicinity of the surf, he ordered them to row vehemently straight through the waves. Soon, the kayak grounded into the sand. Grace quickly hopped out and grasped Josh, getting him to the shore. Her oar plopped into the water, and she bent to fish it out. Just then, a rogue wave came up from behind, hurling her face first into the shallow waves. She bobbed up quickly, spitting the salt water from her mouth and pushing soaked tendrils from her face. She looked at him expectantly.

"Your leash was loose." He held up an empty oar wrap and shrugged.

Feeling her knotted hair, she fit his cap back on her head. "McDonald's, here we come!"

ಸಃ

Grace felt like a wet rat. After she'd shimmied out of her wetsuit, she was still covered in a light film of salt and sand. Still, nothing could wipe the ear-to-ear grin from Josh's face, so it had all been worth it. Trying to get a brush through her tangled web of hair, she sported nominal success and finally gave up, throwing her make-up bag back into her purse. Her appearance mattered little to the bulky fireman, anyway. Her soul turned him off. *Doesn't matter,* she thought to herself. *The likes of Michael Kingston wouldn't be seen with the woman at the well.*

She pictured little Emily Jensen—the petite kindergarten teacher with the gentle, pure nature. If there was only a way Grace could transport herself back in time, to get married first, and build a proper home for Josh. Why hadn't she thought things through? Gone with her first instinct and fled from temptation?

She opened the door, and Josh and Mike waited for her with matching smiles. "Dinner! Dinner!" They chanted together.

She propped her fist on her hip. "It's about time both of you learned a lady is worth waiting for."

"I agree." Mike's eyes met hers, and he quickly looked away. "Let's go, Sport. Our feast awaits."

After a short drive back to Cannery Row, they picked a quaint, family-friendly seafood restaurant. Grace's mouth watered at the delectable menu. Shrimp, halibut, crab. . .she licked her lips at such a decision. She usually just had to contemplate if she wanted fries with her order.

The prices on the menu caused her heart to beat quickly. She hoped her credit card would allow for this meal. She looked to Mike, who sat beside Josh, telling him about all the fish they might try. He caught her looking at him, and she worried he would know how her breathing increased in fear over the bill.

As if his God gave him some type of sign, he dropped his menu. "You know, I think I recognize this restaurant's logo from something. He leaned forward, grasping his black wallet and took out his aquarium tickets, scanning them. "Well, look at that. There's a coupon for half off dinner here. I knew I remembered that logo from somewhere." He tossed the ticket on the table.

Grace wanted to reach over and kiss him. She released a breath, and watched Josh's hair sway in the breeze. She lifted her menu again with relief, studying her choices with renewed faith.

"Josh, I really want you to try some seafood." Mike leaned over showing Josh the menu. This one didn't have pictures, so Josh took Mike's word. "We'll just let you eat the bread and nibble off our plates. Hamburgers are nine dollars here, and I could buy you a good part of a cow for that. We'll do ice cream after dinner. Okay?"

Josh happily agreed because Mike suggested it. Grace had little doubt if Mike suggested Josh eat the tire from his truck for dinner, Josh would have acquiesced.

The waitress came, asking about drink orders, and Grace rejoiced in the fact that Mike didn't drink. Grace also declined, and they each ordered a soda. She ordered a pasta salad for dinner, without the luxury or cost of seafood and Mike ordered the affordable special: baked salmon. Looking at the prices, she noticed he selected the other least expensive meal on the menu.

"Well, are we ready?" Mike said after their meals were finished and cleared away by the server.

"Yes," Grace opened the leather wallet to find the bill and marveled at the actual outcome. It was barely more than a fast food tab. She smiled gratefully to Mike, and he winked at her. "Thank you."

Mike shrugged. "For what? Eating a great meal with a beautiful woman and her son? Anytime." He laughed. For the moment he'd forgotten she was Grace Brawlins, single mother, former Christian, and she basked in the moment.

After dinner, Josh slumped forward, asleep in his carseat for the long drive home. Grace tried to fill the awkward silence.

"I never thought I'd enjoy kayaking."

"I didn't know you did enjoy it." He turned and grinned. Somehow she knew she'd remember that smile against the backdrop of the fading Monterey Bay, forever.

"I did, Mike. Really. I don't understand why you've taken such an interest in Josh, but I do appreciate it."

"How can you question me? Your son has an awesome little personality. He just makes people want to be around him." He looked forward, and she watched his profile with interest. He had a masculine nose, strong, but not too obvious. A thin, open smile always showed his perfect, white teeth. He might have starred in toothpaste commercials if he weren't saving cats for his day job.

"Mike, you have a lot going for you. You have no responsibilities other than your job; you're not bad to look at." She looked out the window when she said this. "And taking on a kid with Josh's issues is just admirable. Especially for a religious type."

"What is it you have against Christians, anyway?"

She contemplated the question. What didn't she have against them was a better question. Deciding he deserved honesty, she went on, "I wasn't always this way. I tried to take Josh to church a couple times when he was young. I could have used the support."

"But?"

"But there was no Sunday School class for me because they didn't consider me appropriate in a singles' class when I had a child, and the young marrieds didn't want me to tempt their husbands." Grace shrugged. "So eventually I just stayed home."

"I'm sorry that happened to you."

And Grace thought he truly was.

"A deaconess was sent to my house to counsel me for my past sins. God may have forgiven me, but His people didn't.

My childhood experiences weren't distant memories, but all too real in the church. I didn't return, and they didn't call me. I figured I'd been right all along. If you don't have your perfection card punched and your floral dress on Sunday morning, don't show up. That's the way it is, huh?"

"You can't judge God by His people—at least not all of the time."

"Then what's the point?"

"To get to know God, Grace. That's the point." He took a hand from the steering wheel for emphasis.

"God knows where I am if He wants me." Grace shrugged.

"He does want you, Grace. And He wants Josh too." Mike shook his head. His chest heaved up and down. "If you're interested, go to the Bible, not people. People will always let you down. I'm sure I will if you give me long enough."

"Did you let Miss Jensen down?"

"Pretty much."

"Well, Fireman Mike, you Christians have some type of club I just don't understand, and quite frankly, I don't want to be a part of. How long did you date Emily?" She moved to safer waters where she wouldn't have to answer any more uncomfortable questions. She'd lost her Christian club card long ago, and there was no going back.

"Emily and I dated for two months. Just before Christmas, I met Josh when I'd help her after school. Josh was always hovering like a bee around her door."

Grace frowned. "He was supposed to be in day care."

"The day care lets them out on the schoolyard when school finishes. Josh just wanted a little extra attention, no big deal."

Grace looked to her hands, clasped so tightly her knuckles were white. "Josh didn't have any friends." It was a statement, not a question.

"He's a slow bloomer, Grace. He'll find his way."

"Will he?" She looked back to her sleeping son. His mouth dangled open, and he breathed loudly.

"He'll bloom. I know it, as sure as I know how to rescue a cat from a tree."

"He's never done anything like today, Mike." Grace smiled from her heart. "He was captain of our kayak."

"Is that a thank you?"

"It is," she admitted. "You'll make a fine dad someday. I think you should call Emily again. Maybe you two will work it out."

The traffic slowed, and Mike turned toward her. "Maybe we will."

She sucked in a deep breath. "She's a fool if she doesn't." *A big fool.*

seven

The door closed, and the lights went on in the Brawlinses' home. Mike rested his head on his steering wheel. Why did this feel so right? He had no claim to this small family, no reason to feel drawn to them. They weren't his responsibility. He looked up to the heavens, searching for an answer.

Why couldn't he make things work with a good Christian woman like Emily? His heart raced at the burden he felt for the Brawlins family. Grace's innocent eyes and full lips sent his heart racing. So much so, he had to avoid her direct gaze, like the sun. He laughed at his romantic notion. He'd just been dumped by Emily. Catching his breath, Mike realized that must be it. He just felt his loneliness. The fact was, nobody waited for him at the end of each day.

He looked at the cottage again and shook his head. Grace wasn't a Christian, and no matter how he might desire it, there were no guarantees. With Grace's anger toward religion in general, it was almost ensured she would never believe. He forced the thought away, yet reality bubbled to the surface. How many men had fallen away while trying to convert a woman? He mentally counted the ones he knew.

His cell phone jolted him from his mind's wanderings. "Hello. Mike Kingston."

"Mike? It's Emily."

Her name should have caused him a reaction, but it didn't. Only mild curiosity as to why she called. That much occurred when a new telemarketer broke into his dinner. "Hi, Emily."

She stammered to find words. He hadn't made it easy for her. "I've had some time to think about Josh and his mother."

"And?"

"I'm sorry about Josh—what I said, I mean. He's a nice kid. I shouldn't have faulted you for spending the day with them." She hesitated a bit. "How was your day, by the way?"

"It was long but worth it. Josh had a great time."

"What about Miss Brawlins?" Her tone irritated him, but he knew accountability would do him good, even if he resented it.

"She had a good time too, I believe. But then with Josh so happy, it would have been hard for her to be disappointed."

"I bet."

Mike let out an annoyed sigh. "I offered to spend time with Josh and *you*, if you'll remember correctly. That was my preference."

"It wasn't my preference, Mike. I've talked with Jared at the station house. He agrees with me."

"About what?" Mike snapped.

"That you have no business witnessing to a single woman. Jared agrees."

"He said that?"

"He didn't have to," Emily said.

"You said it for him?" Mike took in a deep breath, held it for five seconds, and released it to calm down. "Emily, if you'll ask Miss Brawlins to church, I'll continue to see Josh on my own. I don't think Grace would have any objections to that now."

"Are you really that naïve?"

Mike sat back in his truck. "Yeah, maybe I am." He loosened the shirt around his collar. Suddenly, his truck felt stifling. Rolling down the window, he squelched the desire to run, to get away from this noose Emily wanted to place gently about his neck. "I have training in Los Angeles next week. I'll be gone. Maybe you could ask Grace then."

"Maybe I could," she said coldly. "What are you training for?"

"Radioactive emergencies. It's put on by the Department of Energy, and with California's electricity crisis, we're trying to be proactive in the department."

"I'm glad your career is still important to you."

"Yes, it is. I'm on early in the morning, so if that's all you have for me."

"I'm praying for you," Emily practically shouted.

"Thanks," he said absently and started his truck to head for home. If second thoughts ever haunted him, they were long gone now. Emily's heart felt hard to him. Hard and bitter, just the way Grace felt all Christians were. Mike sniffed aloud. He hadn't been on the other side of Christianity. Maybe Grace had a point.

❧

Although worn out and achy from kayaking, Grace returned to work Thursday. She had a skip to her walk, and her coffee tasted richer than usual. Brushing powder on her skin, she noticed her tanned face didn't speak of a miserable day with Josh on suspension. *Thank goodness I told Mr. Falk the truth about my absence.* Grace thought she practically glowed.

Up and ready with a seashell for Show and Tell, Josh sat on the sofa, watching cartoons, and dutifully waited for Grace to finish her coffee. She kissed him good-bye in the house, as she always did to prevent his mortification at school, and they drove the familiar route.

❧

Her office, set in the center of venture capital firms, actually relaxed her. The familiar trickling waterfalls and elaborate water gardens gave peace and serenity to her. It was one of the reasons she'd taken this job as a paralegal for an arbitration specialist.

Mr. Falk smiled as she entered, "Good morning, Grace. How was your day with Josh?"

"Great."

"I have some time this morning, if you're ready for your deposition."

"Now?"

"No time like the present." He opened a hand toward the conference room, and Grace entered, her heart pounding in her ears. "You won't have time to get nervous this way."

"Want to bet?"

He turned on the tape recorder that sat ready in the center of the table and took out his notes. "When did you first meet Lyle Covington?"

"When I was twenty-one and fresh out of college. I was a legal intern at his father's firm." Grace fidgeted in her chair. If she didn't like this line of questioning, she knew it could only get worse. She drew in a deep breath, trying to separate herself from the questions.

"When did you begin to see Mr. Covington on a social level?"

This felt like telling her grandfather secrets, and she thought she might hyperventilate. She took another deep breath. "We often went out to lunch, and even dinner, after long days at the office. Then, there was a Christmas party in 1994."

"How long did your relationship last?" He looked at her over his glasses, then finally looked back to his notes.

"Maybe six months." She crossed her legs.

"When did it end?"

"After the Christmas party. I drank this great-tasting fizzy soda." Grace grappled with her hands. "It was actually champagne, and I wasn't quite myself by the end of the evening." She looked into Mr. Falk's furrowed brows. "I wasn't used to alcohol. I went home to Lyle's apartment with him."

"Did he force you back to his apartment?"

"No." Grace shook her head. "If you know Mr. Covington, he's quite charming, and he doesn't have need to force people into anything. They willingly consent."

"Did you—"

Grace cut him off. "Yes. We consummated the relationship that night." She clutched her hair, twirling it nervously.

"And then?" Mr. Falk's eyebrows lifted.

"Nothing. He had all he wanted, and he lost interest. When he found out about Josh, he gave me a check and the name of a doctor who performs—" Grace stopped. "A doctor who kills babies. His father fired me for lewd behavior, and Lyle shipped off to Boston for a laywers' Masters' program to help the firm bolster its case law clientele."

"Have you spoken with him since?"

Grace nodded. "Twice. Once when I had Josh." Grace looked at the window and focused on the waterfall. "He was the most beautiful baby I'd ever seen, Mr. Falk. I instantly fell in love, and I was naïve enough to believe Lyle would too. I called him to tell him his son was born. He hung up on me."

"And the second time?"

"He just called this week. I saw in the paper he was getting married. He either called for a last fling or to be sure I wouldn't make any waves. I don't know which."

"Grace, I'm sorry, but I must ask this because Lyle's attorneys will most certainly bring it up."

"My personal life." Grace let out a short, uncomfortable laugh.

"He will most likely make you out to be a woman of loose character. It's a standard practice in such cases—anything that helps to put off the actual court-ordered demand for a paternity test."

"That Christmas party was my personal life, Mr. Falk."

"Are you certain?"

"Absolutely. God gave me Josh when I didn't deserve him. I wasn't going to give Him any reason to take him away."

Mr. Falk leaned back. "Grace?" He shook his head. "God doesn't work that way."

"Oh, yes. I know all about His punishment to fit the crime. Justice in God's world is not one I would mess with again. If that fear helps me in the courtroom, so be it." Grace stood. "Are we done for the day? I don't think I can take more now."

"We're done, Grace." Mr. Falk wore a frown unlike any she'd seen on his usually smiling face. In fact, Grace thought he looked capable of crying. She bolted for the door, rushed to the bathroom, and splashed cold water on her face. She felt ill but forced the feeling away.

"This is for Josh," she told the mirror. "So Josh won't have to wear hand-me-downs and sneakers that are too big for him. So kids won't make fun of him and giggle behind his back. Don't be selfish, Grace!" She had the sudden urge to call Fireman Mike and pour out her aching heart. Grace didn't know how she would manage keeping a smile on her face during her days in court. It was bound to get ugly. For the first time in Josh's six years, she wished she could call her parents.

Lyle was not one to part with money easily, and certainly not for the likes of her, a "guttersnipe," as he'd once called her. The fact that he was marrying only made things worse. Grace braced for defeat. Her name was about to be dragged to the lowest parts of the sewer system. Lyle wasn't about to admit his fling with a paltry legal assistant resulted in a child, and she knew he wouldn't let Josh stand in the way of his future.

❧

Mike wandered the aisles of the grocery store while his comrades stood in line at the espresso shop at the front of the store. He gathered the ingredients for dinner, hoping they'd make it through the line without a call. The fresh scent of sourdough bread permeated the air, challenging anyone to leave the store without a loaf.

He dropped a package of chicken into a basket on top of the fresh seasonings and headed toward the checkout. A car alarm wailed in the parking lot, echoing through the store each time the door opened. Jared waved from the Starbuck's line, and Mike relented to the powerful call of bread, running back to the bakery for a French loaf. Squeezing the still-warm bread, it collapsed easily between his grasp. *Perfect,* he thought.

"You through feeling the bread?" Jared stood beside him. "You need a girlfriend, Man." He laughed, slapping Mike on the back.

"Speaking of which, what did you say to Emily last night?"

"She's just worried about you, Mike. Says you spent the whole day with that single mom."

"And her son."

"So what's going on?"

"Nothing more than was going on yesterday. Josh needs me, Jared. I told Emily what she might do at school to make things easier on the kid. She hasn't taken any of my advice, nor has she listened to Grace's suggestions for Josh. It's just easier to believe he's a troublesome kid than to try and lift him out of it."

"You sound awfully passionate about this kid. Don't you

think you're overly involved?"

"Maybe I am, but what's the harm in that? You know where my faith is. You want to hold me accountable? Hold me accountable, but don't fall for Emily's fake concern. It's nothing more than paltry jealousy."

"Mike, what are you talking about? Emily is about as sweet as they come."

"Emily is sweet as long as things go her way. Have you discovered that about her? Because I have, Jared, and I'm just not interested in playing her games anymore. Emily's not even concerned about my life so much as she's concerned about hers. It's fine that we're not together, but it's not fine if I'm with someone else."

"She's just concerned. You are spending a lot of time with a non-Christian."

"No." Mike shook his head while Jared sipped his iced coffee. "Don't buy it. If Emily were concerned, she'd listen to a parent's requests."

"You ain't the kid's father. She's got a right to be concerned. I understand you want to help out, but how far can you take it?"

Mike clenched his jaw. "I don't know, but I'm sick of hearing from Christians about how the unsaved aren't my problem. They're your problem too. Ever heard of the Great Commission? What would happen if we all just sat idly by, waiting for the most convenient witnessing opportunity to wander our way?"

Jared shrugged.

"Oh, look, there's one now. She's wearing a cross, why don't you go tell her about Jesus. She looks easy."

"Come on, Mike. This isn't like you. What's going on?"

"Truthfully? No woman has ever made me feel like Grace

Brawlins. When she blinks her blue eyes at me, I'm captivated. I want to do anything I can to make her life special, to make her feel loved."

Jared scratched the back of his head. "This is serious."

"I feel like I've known her for a lifetime. I've never let my emotions get to me like this. I'm a rational thinker."

Jared laughed. "Women can take any resemblance of rationality we have and twist it to their will. When we're under their spell, it's magical." He clicked his tongue. "But Grace isn't a Christian, Mike, and I will hold you accountable for that. Whatever you're feeling may not be from the Lord."

"I'm sure it probably isn't, and that's what I hate. How can I love her, show her Christ's love without getting in too deep?"

"Maybe you can't." Jared shrugged.

Mike whipped the basket over his elbow and strutted toward the register. Something made him stop, and he turned to see a man drop his groceries. They landed with a clatter at his feet. The sound of breaking glass echoed in the cereal aisle. Just as the man clutched his chest, Mike dropped his own basket, sprinting to the man's side before he fell to the ground.

"My arm!" the man groaned before suddenly losing consciousness. Jared was at Mike's side in a second, calling for backup and supplies. Mike gently lowered the well-dressed man to the floor, checking his vital signs and scrutinizing his color, going into action naturally, like a bodyguard for a great politician.

Finely-groomed with expensive shoes and aftershave, the older man appeared strong and healthy. Devoid of a wedding ring, Mike wondered if the man had a family. Did anyone care that he was having heart failure in the middle of the cereal aisle? Mike blinked. *Would anyone care if I did?* The man's chest ceased its natural rise and fall, and Mike loosened the man's silk tie. He listened for respiration but heard nothing. The man's ankles were thick and fluid-filled.

Mike started resuscitation, with Jared counting off the seconds. Though either one of them could have done this in their sleep, there was something comforting about the sound of the numbers.

As natural as saving a life was, it never became routine. One couldn't help but think about the life this person lived. Would he get another chance? Had he made peace with his family? Only God knew those answers in the midst of procedure, and neither Mike nor his comrades ever lost respect of that.

"I've got a pulse!" Mike called, relieved he wouldn't have to shock the heart. "You're going to be all right," he said gently. Whispering assurance was a vital part of recovery. He checked the pulse again. Although it was weak, it was steady. The man's eyes fluttered open, focusing on Mike.

"Thank you," he croaked.

"You fight. That's thanks enough for me." Mike squeezed the man's hand and felt a lump in his throat rise. Compared to life and death, everything else paled.

An ambulance arrived shortly, taking over and transporting the man to the local hospital only two minutes away. Mike thought the man had a good chance for recovery.

Mike picked up his groceries, putting them back into the basket. Everything seemed in order, except the bread, which lunged out of its protective paper coating.

Kyle Meinrich, a fellow comrade and captain, slapped him on the back. "Good work today."

Jared agreed. "Do you know who that was?"

Mike finished up his silent prayer. "Who?"

"Travis Mann." They said in unison.

"He started Mann Graphics," Jared said, naming the biggest local producer of Hollywood movie effects.

"Then a lot of people care what happens to him." Mike smiled, happy the man wouldn't be alone as he recovered.

"What?" Kyle asked.

"When I saw he didn't have a ring, I wondered if anyone cared that he was here in the store having a cardiac arrest. You know, a wife, children."

Kyle took him aside. "Mike, your value doesn't come from how many people show up at your funeral. Since when did you start being so morbid?"

Since no one really cares if I die, Mike thought. He focused on his captain's piercing gaze. "How is it morbid to think how my work will affect others?"

"Mike, I think you need some time off."

Mike's eyes flashed. He'd heard this speech before, and it was never a good thing for the recipient. "I'm going to the Department of Energy training next week."

"No." Kyle fingered his black collar. "I mean a real vacation, complete with relaxation and peace from the rescue business."

"I'll take one when I get back. The men are all off for their kids' spring break. I'll go after that."

"You've been taking on too many people's shifts. I don't want you trading for the next six months. Do you understand?"

"But, Captain, the men need the weekends with their families. I don't care. I don't have anywhere to be."

"I'm writing it up to make it official, and I've got my eye on you." Kyle's cheek clinched, and Mike felt duly reprimanded.

Jared came beside him, putting an arm around him. "He's right, you know."

"You think I'm going crazy too?'

"I think it's hard not to go crazy in this job. We've seen death in the worst ways possible. How do you not think about that?"

"By concentrating on the afterlife and praying they made a decision for Christ," Mike offered.

"Perfectly spoken by someone who keeps forgetting to live his own life."

"Just because Emily dropped me does not mean my life is over. I've been dumped before, you know. Lots of times."

"Yes, but now you're taking on this family you barely know. You're sacrificing Emily Jensen for them, and you're playing with fire by escorting a gorgeous blond under the guise that her son needs a role model. I know Mike Kingston knows better than this."

"I don't feel crazy. Why is everyone treating me that way?" Mike carried the groceries with Jared at his side.

"You think what happened to your father will happen to you, but you can't know that." Jared paid for the groceries. "And you can't force things to be different."

"Want to bet?" Mike clenched his teeth. "Just watch me."

eight

Mike walked the pale green hallway, scanning the numbers along each room. Kyle had taken him off duty for the next three days, as though he was some type of mental case. Mike still shook his head at the thought. He could feel the angst of Jim Barrow, a father who would miss an important little league game over this suspension. Mike shoved his hand in his pocket and finally found room 304.

He peeked into the room and saw the patient sleeping peacefully. No visitors sat in the chairs, only a bodyguard at the door. Mike flashed his badge and a smile and was nodded through the door. Entry accomplished. He couldn't help but smile. In Silicon Valley, high tech gurus were the rock stars of yesterday.

He sat in the hard chair alongside the bed and watched the patient's chest rise and fall steadily. Mike leaned back in the chair and waited. Within five minutes, the man's eyes blinked open, and he smiled.

"Well, if it isn't the last face I thought I'd ever see. Does that mean I'm dying again?"

Mike laughed. "I'm glad you got another crack at this life."

"Serves me right for doing my own shopping. I can never find anyone who knows how to pick the right apple." He held his hand in the air, like the evil stepmother in *Sleeping Beauty*. Mike could almost hear the cackle. "They have to have a crown. Is that too hard to understand? Crown equals sugar." He held up his hands, his fingers tensed in a clutch.

Mike tried to force away his surprise. If the man got this tense over his apples, no doubt he was ripe for a heart attack. "Maybe you could get a picture. Sometimes it's easier to translate what we mean in pictures."

"Did you come for your reward?" He raised an eyebrow.

"I did, and I've received it in full. You're alive and well."

Travis Mann gave a derisive laugh. "I'm worth more to you that way, I would imagine."

Mike stood and brushed off his sleeve. "Well, Mr. Mann, it might interest you to know, I cannot accept payment for doing my job." Mike guiltily remembered the Aquarium tickets. He should never have taken them. This was just the kind of instance where gratitude might hurt his reputation. "If you care to bake me an apple pie, I can accept that." He squared his shoulders and walked toward the door. "Or if you wish to donate something to the fire staff, that's all right, but I won't be able to accept your cash gift." Mike chuckled.

"Wait a minute." Mr. Mann's eyes narrowed and he scrutinized Mike from head to toe. "No need to get uptight. I didn't mean anything by my words. I'm a businessman, Mr.—"

"Mike Kingston." He walked toward Travis's extended hand and shook it.

"I just assume everyone else is a businessman too. I forget there are some of you soft hearts still left in the world. Some of you who just want to do good and move on."

"Be thankful there are." Mike winked.

"Touché." Travis fiddled with his tubing, trying to wrestle free of its grip upon him. "What about a dinner invitation? Can you accept that?"

Mike shrugged. "It doesn't appear that we have anything in common, Mr. Mann. I came by to see that you were all right, that's all. You don't owe me a thing."

"I disagree." Travis shook his head. "I owe you the rest of my life, as do my children."

"You owe that to God. Just make yourself worthy of His gift."

"I married a young woman recently. She's twenty-six."

Mike forced his widened eyes to look away.

"I know what you're thinking, Mike Kingston. I hope you're not a gambling man because that poker face of yours is bad, indeed." He opened the drawer beside him, and pulled out some papers. "I'm sixty-four, in case you haven't mentally calculated yet."

"How old are your children? If you don't mind my asking."

"Twenty-eight and thirty-three."

Mike nodded, trying to appear unfazed, when he actually wanted to throttle the man. He looked at Travis's elegant, silver hair and the crimson silk robe worn as though he were royalty. The sight of the man sent a wave of sickness through Mike's already tight stomach. A twenty-six year old could be his granddaughter.

"Well, I'm glad you'll make the most of your time." Mike turned on his heel.

"Now wait a minute." Travis opened the folder on his lap. "This here's my will. My wife was quite thrilled it hadn't been updated after our marriage."

Mike held up his palm. "Mr. Mann, I am really glad you've made it, but this is none of my business, and if you knew my history, you probably wouldn't be sharing it with me."

"Nonsense. I'm sharing it with me, because you didn't just save my life, you saved my children's inheritance. How long have I been in here, Mr. Kingston?"

"Since yesterday, Sir."

"And it turns out my little wife has already been to see her lawyer." Travis shook his head, his heart clearly bent on revenge. "I've rewritten the will, and I'd like you to witness it, Mr. Kingston. Since you're here, I think it's quite hysterical that such a good-looking young man should sign my wife's financial demise. She seems to have an eye for the poor, brawny types. Well, she's not going to live on my quarter."

"I'd rather not sign any such thing, Mr. Mann. I'm sure you have a few family members or friends who warned you about this woman *before* you married her."

"As a matter of fact, I did."

"I'm just glad your children aren't going to pay the price for your temporary foolishness for the rest of their days. They deserve the inheritance." *I'm sure it's the only part of you they want anymore,* Mike added to himself. He felt his jaw twitch.

"You certainly speak your mind for not knowing me from Adam."

Mike had already crossed the line; there was no sense retreating now. "I think the fact that your children are older than your wife speaks for itself, Mr. Mann."

"Prejudices, prejudices. I thought she was madly in love with me." Travis shrugged. "I'm young for my age. I still ski, keep fit, look good for my age. Why wouldn't I believe she was in love with me?"

"Did you ever ask yourself if you were a poor man, would she still love you?"

"No, I never did. Successful men are attractive to women, Mr. Kingston. That's why the older ones can still get the young gals."

Mike couldn't hold back his laughter. "Is that what you think? You, who started one of the most successful companies in the country, do you really believe that the success is what attracts these women? Not the money?" Mike slapped his leg, unable to maintain his mirth.

"Success and money go hand in hand, Mr. Kingston. I'm glad this is so hilarious to you, but it's the end of my marriage. Do you find that funny?" Travis's steely gray eyes met Mike's own, and all humor left.

"No, I don't find that the least bit funny. I guess I'm just shocked you're surprised. What did you expect to have in common with this woman?"

"I want to ski, I want to mountain climb. How many old ladies my age would be able to do all that?"

"I bet there are quite a few. Did you ever bother looking for one?" *I know my father didn't.*

"You're an upstart, you know that?"

At the first hint of anger in Travis's voice, Mike got nervous. He didn't want to upset the man in any way, and when the heartbeat beeps quickened, Mike knew he'd made a mistake in coming. "Mr. Mann, I don't mean you any disrespect. You've accomplished a lot in your lifetime, and you deserve to be rewarded for that. I let my own history cloud my opinion. I'm sorry."

Mr. Mann's face relaxed. "No need to apologize, Mr. Kingston. I respect you for saying your piece. It's not many who will tell me what they really think. I like that in a man."

Mike thrust his hand forward. "It was a pleasure to meet you, Sir. I'm glad you're all right."

"You ever need a job, you come see me."

"Thanks, Mr. Mann, but I'm happy in my current one. Take care of yourself, and write your will first. . .before the next marriage."

Travis laughed heartily. "Will do."

Mike walked out of the hospital room and leaned against the wall, chastising himself for not sharing the Lord with a man who so desperately needed Him. He said a prayer for Travis Mann and waved good-bye to the security guard.

ᶻᵃ

Grace finished the day's work, sorted through her paperwork, and locked her desk. She waved to Mr. Falk as she exited. Her stomach swirled at the sight of the older man. It didn't feel right, having her boss know so much about her personal life. But what choice was there? She and Josh lived in one of the most expensive areas in the country with only Grace's small salary to support them. There had to be more for him. She would see to it that Lyle Covington didn't buy one more sports car on her son's money.

The trickle of the atrium waterfall instantly soothed her, and she smelled the sweet scent of grassy hills that bordered the office. She closed her eyes and just let the peace wash over her. Just one moment when she had no worries, nothing on her mind, just her senses filled by the beauty around her. She savored it.

She opened her eyes and faced her broken-down Ford in the parking lot. The peace was shattered. The short, scenic drive to Josh's school lost its beauty in the bumper-to-bumper traffic she encountered with her car sputtering the entire way.

Josh waited at the school, his little fingers curled through the chain link fence, his knuckles white, as though he'd been there for some time. Grace's heart cinched. How she envied the mothers who picked their children up when school ended. She slammed the door on her Ford and sprinted to the fence where she took his hands in her own.

"I missed you today, Josh."

He blinked rapidly, and she tried to ignore the red in his eyes. "Can we go now?"

"Of course, we can. We have to go by the grocery store.

I'm out of lunchmeat."

"Aw, Mom, I'm tired. Can't we just go home? I'll eat peanut butter tomorrow."

"Okay, Buddy." She unlatched the gate and went toward the portable building to sign her son out. The college students who worked there were stretched out on the sofas while children ran about wildly. They sat upright at the sign of Grace. She tried to still her angry breathing. She scribbled her name, grabbed Josh's backpack, then Josh's hand, and left without a word.

"If we go to the grocery store, can I get some ice cream?"

Grace looked down at his large, brown eyes. The melancholy borne there wouldn't be erased with any amount of ice cream. Grace got into her car, and despair washed over her in a rush. Leaning against the steering wheel, she couldn't fight the tears any longer. Though she was her son's only protector, she was utterly powerless to defend him during the day. She gritted her teeth and raged against Lyle and his selfishness.

"I'm sorry, Mommy. I don't want any ice cream. Peanut butter is good."

Grace whacked the steering wheel. "No, Honey. It's not you. We'll get you some ice cream at the store. We'll get something good for dinner too. Whatever you want."

"I want a Lunchable. With a soda."

"No soda before bed. You'll be up all night, but you can pick a Lunchable with a different drink." Grace pulled her Ford in between two luxury sedans. She could just see the horror in the owners' eyes when they came back to the lot. She stifled a giggle.

"Mom, there's Fireman Mike!" Josh shot out of the backseat and laid on the horn. Grace tried to sink into the seat, but Josh waved vigorously. Fireman Mike had, indeed, seen them, as had everyone else in the shopping center.

He approached the car. Grace caught her breath. She'd forgotten since yesterday just how handsome he was, and she questioned fate for running into him. Being seen by Mike Kingston at the end of such an emotional day was like going on the Oprah show on the worst hair day of your life.

"Hi, Grace! Hey, Josh! What are you two up to?"

"Grocery shopping." Josh crinkled his nose. "What are you doing?"

"Well, I'm living in a typical bachelor pad today. My milk is sour, and my lettuce is wilting, so here I am. How was your day, Grace?" He opened the door for her and extended his hand to help her up.

Inwardly, Grace cringed at the ripped upholstery and faded dashboard after riding in Mike's elegant truck a few days before. "I've had better."

"Me too. Let's just say I'm glad I had the fun of our adventure to live on today."

Grace stared into his eyes, his laugh lines worn into the edges. The ever-chipper Christian had disappeared behind a pained expression.

"I'm sorry your day was bad, Mike." Instinctively, she grasped for his hand, and he clutched hers in return. There were no sudden movements, no disgust apparent in his grip.

"Thank you." Mike took his hand and placed it on Josh's shoulders. "What about you, Sport? How was your day?"

"Stupid. I told the kids I spent yesterday with you at the aquarium and kayaking, and they didn't believe me. They said I lied and that I just was pretending 'cuz I got no daddy."

"You tell them I had no daddy either, Josh. That's what we have in common."

"Did you ever get a daddy?" Josh asked.

Grace nearly fainted against the car. She hoped Josh wasn't about to ask the gorgeous fireman if he'd like to apply for the position. "Josh! That's none of our business."

Mike bent over. "The truth of the matter is, I always had a father, but I never had a daddy. Now I have God, and He's the best daddy ever."

Grace couldn't even be mad at him for going against her wishes on religion. Mike meant no harm. It was obvious he only wanted to help Josh. Maybe he would benefit from some of the social programs at Mike's church. If the kids saw him with Mike, maybe they might be more inclined to include him at school. "I don't mind if you take Josh on Sunday, if you're free."

Mike blinked several times before speaking. "Really?"

"Really."

"Was your mommy nice?" Josh asked.

"She was the best." Mike stood tall, meeting Grace's eyes again. "Well, maybe the second best."

Josh took both their hands, connecting them together in a shared bond of love for a precious little boy. They embarked on a grocery shopping adventure that Grace found herself hoping would never end.

nine

"Hello?" Grace dropped the groceries on the table, breathing audibly as she answered the phone.

"Miss Brawlins?"

"Yes, who is this?"

"It's Emily Jensen, Josh's teacher."

Grace's heart sank. "Oh, Miss Jensen, is Josh in trouble?"

"No, no, nothing like that. This call is of a personal nature. I hope you don't mind. Is this a good time?"

Grace tried to concentrate in her confusion while she watched Josh get himself his Lunchable and set himself down for a less-than-healthy dinner. "Sure. What can I do for you, Miss Jensen?"

"I wanted to invite you to church this Sunday. Well, you and Josh."

Grace felt more riddled with questions than before. What was this sudden interest in her getting religion that everyone seemed to have? Now, Miss Jensen too. And what about church and state? Was this woman allowed to invite her to church? Wasn't that going against the Constitution or something?

Grace finally found her tongue. "Fireman Mike already asked Josh to church this Sunday. He said he has the day off before leaving for his new training in Los Angeles. I was actually thinking of going with the two of them." Grace thought she heard Miss Jensen's breath catch, and she found herself rattling off an excuse. "I think it might be good for Josh, you know, to have the two of us there."

"We'll be going together, Miss Brawlins. Mike and I. I was calling to invite you with us."

Grace watched Josh, trying to avoid the feelings churning within her. *Jealousy.* Red hot, boiling jealousy. Plain and simple, that's what she felt. An emotion not present within her since she'd found out Lyle was seeing other women at the office before his father could ship him off to his Masters.

"That's very kind of you, Miss Jensen, but I am confident Josh will be in good hands with the two of you."

"Great. You'll have a nice morning to yourself then. Maybe you can treat yourself and a friend to brunch."

"Yes, that sounds nice," Grace pretended, lowering herself into a chair. She didn't have the money to enjoy a brunch out, with or without a friend. She'd probably spend her Sunday morning alone, curled up on the couch with a cooking show, lamenting why she ever gave up precious time with Josh to these strangers.

"Did Mike say what time he'd be picking up Josh? I'll probably just meet him at your house and save him a trip to pick me up."

"He said he'd come at nine."

"You're sure you won't come with us. We usually have a late breakfast or lunch following the service." It wasn't a question. It was more of a statement. "We'll probably get back about one-thirty."

"You know, Miss Jensen, I only get my son nights and weekends, that's a long time for me to be away from him. Maybe—"

"Nonsense. The break will do you good. Mike is always talking about how tired you look. This will give you a chance to rest."

Grace stretched the phone cord to the small mirror at the

back door. Taking a forefinger, she pulled her under eye area, studying the bags. She did look awfully sallow, but it had been a trying day. Didn't Mike understand that? "Well, since it's just this once, I suppose one-thirty will be all right."

"That's right. Just this once. Maybe Josh will get to be a little more friendly with some of the kids attending. That would help him in my class as well."

Grace felt the sting of the comment as though it were a slap across her cheek. "Yes, that would be nice."

"Well, I guess I'll see you Sunday morning. I'll take your address down at the school."

Grace hung up the phone and stared at Josh. His Lunchable stood, a wreckage of plastic and paper, the foodstuff all devoured. "I guess that was pretty good, huh?"

"You're the best, Mom. I'll eat my string beans tomorrow, I promise."

Grace laughed. "I'll remind you tomorrow, you said that."

"I know."

"That was your teacher on the phone. She's going to go with you and Fireman Mike to church this weekend." *The perfect little family.* Grace swallowed hard, forcing back the sick pangs of envy she felt.

"Aw, why? Why is she coming with us? I don't want her coming with us, with her sickening sweet voice." Josh broke into a falsetto, " 'Why, Mike? What a wonderful surprise!' It's really disgusting."

"Where did you learn that word?"

"From the girls at school. I showed them this bug, and they all said that word. But it was really cool, not disgusting. Girls don't know." Josh plopped onto the sofa, crossing his arms.

Grace kissed Josh's head. "Where's your homework?"

"No homework tonight."

Grace breathed a sigh of relief. Homework for a kindergartner was ridiculous, but she tried to be supportive, knowing Josh could only benefit from keeping up with the wealthy set at Los Altos Elementary.

"Can I call Fireman Mike?"

"What for? You just saw him at the grocery store."

"No reason." Josh's brown eyes opened wide, giving every indication he wasn't telling her the truth.

"Fireman Mike has enough to do tonight. You'll see him on Sunday."

"Oh, all right. You like him, right, Mom?"

"Of course I do. He's been very kind to us, and we had a nice time kayaking and at the aquarium."

"No. I mean *like* him. He makes you all funny like Miss Jensen, and I think we need him more. I am going to tell him so."

Grace clutched her pounding heart. "You'll do no such thing, Joshua Blake Brawlins. These ideas of yours are nice, but they are only your imagination. Fireman Mike will marry someone else, maybe Miss Jensen, and have a nice family of his own. We are our family, Josh. I'm sorry Mommy made it that way, but that's the way it is. Go ahead and watch *Rugrats*. I'll be in as soon as I fix myself something to eat and get these groceries put away."

"All right, but you're prettier than her, Mom. Way prettier."

Grace stifled her giggle. "Thank you, Joshua. You made my night." Unpacking the milk and orange juice, Grace couldn't help but hope Mike agreed with her son.

≈

Mike cut up a little cilantro and topped his Chinese chicken salad with the garnish. He took a whiff of the spicy Mexican parsley and inhaled. "Mmm, this is living." The phone rang and broke his reverie.

"Michael Kingston speaking."

"Mike, it's Emily."

The sweetness in her voice reeked of apology, and Mike found himself not in the mood. Emily's heart for his ministry was cold as ice, and suddenly he felt the same way about her. "How are you, Emily? Things going well at school?" He forced his friendliness. He still hadn't forgotten their heated words.

"I did what you asked me to."

"What do you mean?"

"I asked Grace to church."

Mike's hardened emotions softened. "You did? Emily, that's great. What did she say?"

"She wasn't really interested. I think Miss Brawlins has a little animosity toward God."

Mike raked his hair back. How he wished he might help Grace's heart to open toward God. "It has something to do with her parents, though I'm not sure what. Somehow, she's been very hurt by God's people."

"Well, regardless, we can't sow a seed when she doesn't have ears to hear. Shake off our sandals, you know? I told her I'd meet you at her house with Josh, so she wouldn't have any worries on Sunday."

"Great!" Mike let out a deep sigh. "Maybe we can talk her into going with us on Sunday when we see her."

"Sure, sure." Emily cleared her throat. "Listen, can we do lunch after Sunday school? I feel like we haven't connected at all, you know?"

Mike couldn't explain his hesitation, but he stalled for time, unsure why he regretted the idea of spending time with Emily. . .sweet kindergarten teacher Emily, a Christian since childhood. Why would he rather be with a single mother who didn't know Jesus?

"With Josh, of course," Emily clarified.

"Right. Sure, if it's okay with Grace, I'm sure that would be fine. You'll get to spend some more time with him and see why he's such an awesome little boy. Grace has done an incredible job raising him on her own, especially without calling on the Lord. Think how much easier life would be for her, if she only cast her cares on the Lord and resorted to prayer instead of her own will."

"I think if you saw a little more of Josh Brawlins, you might rethink her perfection. The kid has a severe social problem. He has no friends, Mike."

"Maybe it's Los Altos Elementary that has the social problem." Mike clenched his teeth but released them after inhaling a deep breath.

"Mike," Emily said gently, "Joshua is a charming little boy. I'm not denying that. And sure, for a single mother with questionable morals, Grace does a fine job, but Josh is not without problems. He puts on a careful face for you. He's looking for a father, Mike, and I just don't want you to raise his hopes."

Mike felt a stab of guilt. Was he doing that? Raising a little boy's hopes only to crush them in the future? "You're probably right, Emily. I will be careful."

"I've got a full lesson plan tomorrow. I'd best hit the hay a little early."

"Okay, Emily. Thanks for calling, and thanks for calling Grace. Maybe she'll come with us next time."

Mike's gourmet salad sat before him, the freshly roasted chicken from the grocery wafting its scent throughout the whole kitchen. Suddenly and without explanation, he'd lost his appetite. He grabbed his Bible and began reading, looking for solace in the Scriptures.

～

Grace tucked Josh into bed and kissed his forehead. "Bad day today, huh? Let's hope tomorrow is better."

"Why don't we pray it will be better?"

Grace sat back. "Josh," she said quietly, "I know Fireman Mike is a neat man, and I know he believes in God." Grace wished there was some way to avoid the conversation, but their differences were bound to come out sooner or later. "That's okay for Fireman Mike, Honey, but I think we need to concentrate on tangible things. Do you know what that means?"

Josh shook his head, his eyes wide. "No."

"It means that we depend on things we can see and touch." Grace clapped her hands in the air. "Wishing for things is fine, but expecting them and believing some big, invisible god in the sky is going to get them for us is just not healthy. We have to work for things to make them happen."

"Wishing is just wishing, Mom. You wish for something, maybe it will happen, maybe it won't, but praying for something is telling God."

"Josh, I don't believe God is there for me. I'm sorry, Buddy. I know that's hard for you to hear."

"I do. And I'm praying for Fireman Mike to be my daddy."

Grace was startled to hear her son's words. She had never mentioned God other than to tell Josh how most people based their view on an almighty in the sky and told stories from an old book about who this God was. Where did he get such ideas? Mike simply hadn't spent that much time with him.

"Fireman Mike is not going to be your daddy, Josh." Grace brushed her son's bangs away from his eyes. "You need a haircut." Mentally, she calculated where she would get the eight dollars she'd need for that.

"All you have to do is ask Jesus into your heart. That's what Mike says. Why can't you do that, Mom? Then he could marry you, and I could have a father, and Miss Jensen could find someone else—someone not as nice as Mike because she doesn't deserve him."

Grace got up from the bed, bending to pick up Legos and assorted toys that littered Josh's bedroom. "That's not for us to decide. I'm not asking Jesus or anyone else into my heart, Josh. Maybe church on Sunday isn't such a good idea for you."

Josh shook his palms, sitting upright. "No, Mom. I'm sorry. I want to go on Sunday, please? Some of the kids in after-school care will be there, and I told them I was coming. If I don't go, they won't believe Fireman Mike and me is friends. They'll laugh at me again."

Grace wondered if Josh had been born differently, into a wealthy family with two parents, if he would have been the popular, cool kid instead of the skinny, fearful child he was. "I'll let you go on Sunday because I promised but no more, Joshua. Fireman Mike needs to go about his business, and we need to move on. We are not getting him as a daddy, and he needs to spend time finding himself a wife or getting engaged to Miss Jensen."

"You'd just let him marry Miss Jensen?" Joshua pointed at her accusingly. "She'll be mean to him, Mom, like she's mean to some of the kids at school. Then, she's all sugary around the principal and Fireman Mike." Josh puckered his lips, imitating kissing sounds. "All you have to do is pray to Jesus. Mike told me!"

"Stop it, Joshua!" Grace felt her voice rising, and she could tell by Josh's reaction, it had indeed reached a higher pitch. She stopped and counted to ten. "Go to sleep." Grace clicked off the light and shut the door.

Josh shouted after her, "Well, I'm gonna keep asking Jesus. You can't stop me, and you can't stop God!"

Grace closed her eyes, and fell backwards against the wall, sliding down until she reached the cold tile floor. She gripped her hair and pulled as tightly as she could, until pain seared through her scalp. "My mother has something to do with this. I don't know how, but that woman will haunt me with her cold, callous religion until the day I die."

Grace sat directly across from the utility room. Dirty laundry covered the floor, and Grace rose, knowing it had to get done. Josh had nothing to wear to school. She started the washer and poured discount detergent into the machine, then added Joshua's jeans and broadcloth, button-up shirts. All his clothes were the finest designer labels. She didn't know where they'd come from. Someone had left them on the doorstep, but she wasn't about to thumb her nose at good, sturdy clothes. The shirt she held in her hand probably cost thirty dollars or more, and it was barely worn. Tossing it into the washer, she closed the lid and headed to the kitchen.

Josh had gotten out of bed and sat at the kitchen table, his little fists holding up his chin. "I don't know why you're mad at God. He didn't get us into this mess."

Grace halted in the doorjamb. "What? I suppose you think I got us into this mess. Is that what you're trying to say?" Grace shook with anger—anger at herself for getting them into this, and anger at her son for figuring it out.

"Mike says God doesn't allow things to happen to His people that won't be good for them later."

"Mike certainly says a lot. When, pray tell, does he tell you all this valuable information?"

"When he comes to afterschool care."

Grace went toward Josh, kneeling on the floor and placing her chin on the table at his eye level. "Mike comes to afterschool care?"

"Not anymore," Josh had a tear in his eye. "He used to come and see Miss Jensen, and then he'd come to afterschool care and see me for awhile, but he doesn't come anymore. That's why I was so sad when you picked me up today."

"Josh, we just had a bad day all around. It will get better, I promise."

"I want to pray for it to get better."

"Josh—"

"Mom, I wondered about God, but you would never answer me. Fireman Mike did."

"Okay, Josh, if it makes you feel better, you pray. I'll hold your hand and close my eyes, and you pray, all right?"

Josh broke into a grin. "Cool." Josh clenched his eyes shut, and Grace watched him through an open eye, but he opened his again to make sure she followed suit. Grace clenched her own eyes shut.

"Go ahead." She sighed.

"Dear Jesus, my mom and I are having a really hard day. We don't want any more bad days, God. Could you give us a good day tomorrow? And could you make Mike my daddy? Amen."

Grace grimaced at his prayer but kissed his forehead, and he ran off to bed without another word. She hoped Mike would marry Miss Jensen quickly. It would squelch any false hopes in Josh. *And me too*, she thought. She pictured Mike in his torn-at-the-knees jeans and his navy fire department T-shirt stretched over his muscular chest. She relived her joy as he held hands with Josh in the grocery store, and ultimately with her. It was the life she imagined for herself—the one she would have been living if she hadn't angered God. She let out a deep sigh. Since when did she become such a daydreamer?

ten

Grace awoke with a start at the sound of the phone. She stumbled toward the kitchen, tripping over the basket of laundry she'd left in the hallway. "Hello," her voice held fatigue. She clutched the phone with both hands. "Hello?"

"Grace?" An unfamiliar woman's voice answered. "This is Kathy Houston. Do you remember me?"

Grace's blurred vision focused on the clock. It was only 9:50 P.M., yet she felt like it was three in the morning. She rubbed her head. "Kathy." She processed the name a few times in her mind. "Yes, we were paralegals together a long time ago."

"Right. Listen, I'm sorry to call so late. It sounds like I woke you, but I wanted to warn you about something."

"Warn me?" Grace shook the sleep from her head.

"I got a call from someone at the old firm. I guess you have some type of suit going against Lyle Covington."

"Already?" Grace's breathing quickened. She had no idea the ball would begin rolling so quickly. She'd only just given her statement. *How on earth?* Mr. Falk wouldn't threaten her case, but who would? "I'm sorry, Kathy, you've thrown me a bit. I wasn't ready for this yet. I thought I'd have more time to prepare. We haven't filed suit yet."

"Grace, I think you remember how our old firm went after a case. That's why I called. I wanted to share what I knew so you could prepare against the machine. I'm not under any oath, and I certainly don't owe any Covington favors."

Grace clutched her stomach, hoping this was some kind of nightmare, but looking around at the pile of unfolded laundry she knew things were exactly as she'd left them before sleep. "What did they ask you?"

"They're looking to harm your reputation. They wanted to know what I knew about your social life during your time at the firm."

Grace doubled over, feeling like she'd been punched. "Did you tell them anything?"

"I told them I remember you dating Lyle and no one else, but then I didn't see much of you socially. We were too busy with the hours at the firm."

Relief flooded her. "I didn't date anyone else, Kathy, just for the record." For some reason, she felt the need to justify herself to Kathy, to anyone who would listen now. She'd been quiet for too long, and Josh had suffered too much.

Kathy, as if reading her mind, continued. "Grace, I don't know if this is what you need to hear right now, but who knows when I'd get the chance to tell you again? I think it might be important to your case."

Grace swallowed. "Do you have a child by Lyle?"

"Oh, heavens, no, Grace. It's nothing like that. It's just that Lyle tried to get me drunk at an office party once. I had been warned by others about him, and I feel really guilty that I never warned you, especially when I learned it eventually cost you your job."

"I knew better than to drink, Kathy. It was my own fault."

"I left the firm shortly after you did, but it always bothered me that I should have warned you." Kathy paused for a moment. "So if you're wondering why you're hearing from me out of the blue, it's because I feel God has given me another opportunity to make things right. I'm warning you now. He's a snake, Grace, and he'll do whatever he can to win this lawsuit. . .whatever it may be."

"He can't win it, Kathy. It's a paternity case, and once I get the court order for him to give DNA evidence, there will be no denying his role in my son's life." Grace squared her shoulders, finally confident in something.

"Be careful, Grace. He'll do whatever it takes to avoid that test. I have no doubt. He'll paint you as a harlot. He'll say you came after him because he is rich. He'll do whatever he can. I know just by the questions they're asking. Remember when we worked on discovery how ruthless the firm was?"

"I remember." Her stomach swirled.

"Grace, tell your lawyer I'm willing to testify that Lyle tried to get me drunk and take advantage of me, and I can probably find a few others who would testify to the same thing. I'll do what I can to help, and we'll force Lyle to take that test and own up to his responsibility."

"Why would you do this?"

"Because I'm a Christian, Grace, and Christians tell the truth. I should have been more forthright seven years ago, then maybe none of this would have happened."

Another Christian. Grace closed her eyes and shook her head. They were like cockroaches, living under every corner and crevice, invading her thoughts and dreams. She pushed away thoughts of her childhood, romantic memories she'd probably embellished over the years due to loneliness. God didn't care anymore. He couldn't.

"I appreciate you calling, Kathy. It couldn't have been easy for you to admit that, but I don't blame you for keeping quiet. Not at all."

"Thank you, Grace. It's just like you to worry about my feelings when you're facing a mountain of trouble."

"Lyle's getting married, Kathy. That's why I'm doing this now. Our son wears hand-me-downs and goes to afterschool care while I work my tail off to provide a home for him. It's just not right, and he is not going to start fresh with some cute little family without paying for the one he already has. Whether or not he wanted Josh, he's responsible for him."

Kathy's voice was clear and soft. "I'm glad you're fighting to establish paternity. It's vital that a man provides financially for the children he creates. But don't let it eat you alive, Grace. I'm sure you're a wonderful mother. You always had the gentlest nature. A lack of finances a child can always get over, but your son is lucky to have you as a mother. Don't forget that."

"Kathy, thank you." A lump formed in her throat. There wasn't a day that went by in which she wondered if she was doing right by Josh. The words of confidence inspired her. "I appreciate you calling out of the blue like this. I won't let Lyle sideswipe me again. I'm ready for the battle." Grace straightened against the wall. Suddenly, she felt as though her armor was ready.

"I'm praying for you, Grace, and I'm in the book if you need anything else. If you need someone to baby-sit or just talk to, please call."

"Thank you, Kathy. Good-bye." Grace placed the receiver back into its cradle. She stared at the phone a minute longer, and steeled herself for the phone call she'd been dreading. Now was as good a time as any. Josh, fast asleep in the room, would be spared her emotions, and since Lyle had already started his inquisition, it seemed fair for Grace to hit them with the news first.

Carefully, she pressed each button, amazed at how time had done nothing to diminish the speed in which she dialed the number. She drew in a deep breath and braced herself against the wall.

"Hello." She heard the familiar voice, the judgment still apparent through thin, pursed lips. Grace could see them, the wrinkles probably now more set by the elder woman's anger. Grace almost hung up, and the harsh tone came back at her. "Hello. Listen, it's late here. You got something to say? Say it."

"Mom." She paused and drew in another breath. "Mom, it's Grace."

Silence greeted her, and Grace just waited. At some point, her mother would have to answer her or hang up. The silent game of cat-and-mouse continued until, finally, Harriet Brawlins spoke, "Are you in trouble again?"

"In a way, yes," Grace answered, almost defiantly.

"Well, your father and I are on a fixed income and—"

"Mom, have I ever asked you for money? Ever?"

"No, but it seems odd you should call out of the blue like this when we haven't spoken for seven years, and so late too. I told your father one day you'd call, in trouble."

"Gracie?" Her father's voice came on the line, and Grace teared at the sound of his comforting voice.

"Daddy?"

"Gracie, what's the matter, Honey? Do you need something? Is Joshua okay?"

Grace was startled at the use of Josh's name. She didn't think her parents even bothered to remember their grandchild's given name. "We're fine, Daddy. I just wanted to tell you both that I am going to court to prove Lyle, Josh's father, should be paying child support. I wanted you to know before anyone called. His firm might call asking questions."

"Your father lost his deaconship at the church over your behavior." Harriet's disappointment in Grace hadn't diminished a bit. "I suppose you didn't think about the wake you left behind."

"I'm sorry about that, Mom, but I thought church was in the business of forgiveness."

Her mother started to speak again, when her father's voice interrupted. "Just never mind about that, Harriet. Your daughter's on the phone. Let her talk."

"Anyway, I just wanted you to know that I didn't live a loose lifestyle, and no matter what Lyle tries to tell you, it's a lie. Joshua is his son, and he needs to support the child."

"You, who became pregnant out of wedlock, are going to tell me you didn't live a loose lifestyle?" Her mother let out that same haunting, rude cackle that brought every hateful feeling back.

Grace pursed her lips, trying with all her might to rein in the emotions that hovered in her throat. "I suppose you would have rather had me take that check from Lyle. Is that what you're saying, Mother? That Joshua would be better off dead because he didn't come into the world your way? That your life, and your deaconship, might have been spared if I'd taken matters into my own hands?" Grace shook with anger, and she wished she could reach through the phone and throttle her mother.

"Gracie!" Her father sounded horrified, and she heard him break into a sob. A heart-wrenching, gasping sob. Grace crumbled, hearing the awful sound of him crying out in his pain.

"You just won't be happy until everyone in your life does everything to your satisfaction, will you, Mother? Well, I've got news for you. Joshua is ten times better than I ever was. He's a delightful child who will probably be a doctor or an engineer or something equally successful, and I relish that you'll take no credit for his success. None." Grace sniffled relentlessly, trying to will her raining tears back. "Because you know what, Mom? I don't care if Josh is perfect, I just want him happy!"

"Stop it, both of you! Gracie, we're sorry. We're so sorry. We were wrong, and we miss you, Darling. We want you to come back home. To come back to your faith."

Grace harbored a bitter laugh. "I don't want anything to do with your religion, and I don't want Josh to either. Because when Josh lets me down, Dad, I'm going to take him in my arms and tell him it's okay—that I love him anyway."

Her father could barely speak. His voice broke in coughing sniffles with every attempt. "Oh, Gracie, we have let you down so." Harriet began to speak when she heard a new side of her husband. "Be quiet, Harriet. Get off the phone if you can't keep your judgment and hateful thoughts to yourself. We've pushed our daughter away long enough!" He coughed again and apparently tried to compose himself. Grace waited patiently, wishing she could hug the man who meant so much to her.

"Daddy."

"Gracie, I remember when you were on my knee at seven. I remember when you asked Jesus into your heart, and I believe with all my heart He still dwells there, if only you'll apologize to Him. Tell Him you'll live your life for Him again. Please don't let our mistakes turn you against God."

"Dad, it's too late. I'm not that little girl anymore. She died when Josh was born."

"You are that little girl to God, Gracie. He'll take all your mistakes, all our mistakes when we own up to them. Don't you want Joshua to know that kind of forgiveness?"

"Joshua is doing just fine on his own strength, Dad."

"He's a nice little boy, Gracie. You've done well with him, but finish the job."

"How do you know anything about Josh, Dad? Maybe I've done a terrible job."

"I've seen you two together, Gracie. I've come down to the Bay Area a few times. I wanted to talk to you, to see you, but I was afraid. I let you down as a dad, and I didn't want to be reminded about that. I didn't want to see your anger vented toward me. I was a coward."

"You were here?" Grace fell against the wall.

"I love you, Gracie. I've been a fool, but that never stopped my love for you or for Josh. I left him clothes on your doorstep. Clothes and a few toys. Did you ever get them?"

Grace always thought those clothes were hand-me-downs, but thinking back, many had shrunk the first time she washed them. The clothes had always arrived just when she didn't know what she was going to do for shoes or jeans. She thought the wealthy of Los Altos had passed their expensive things to Josh. She should have known they wouldn't have thought twice of the resident single mother.

"The clothes have been great, Dad. I don't know how I would have made it without them sometimes."

"Can I meet him, Gracie? You don't have to tell him I'm his grandpa, but can I meet him?"

"Oh, Dad, really? You want to meet him?" Grace grabbed a towel from the laundry basket, then swiped her soaked cheeks.

Her mother harrumphed and hung up the phone. Both Grace and her father ignored the gesture.

"I've wasted seven years of his life, seven years of yours. Forgive me, Gracie. Forgive me." He sounded older, and Gracie wondered if he had aged so much in seven short years.

"I do forgive you, Dad." And she did too. Everything within her longed to be in her father's arms again, to be his little princess and bask in his tales of Jesus and his prayers over her each evening. "I want Josh to know you as Grandpa, Dad."

"I'll earn the title from here on out. I don't want you to worry about this Lyle character, Gracie. I should have protected you seven years ago, and I don't intend to let him hurt my baby again. He'll pay for his son, as he should have done long ago. I'll sell the house if we need money for the lawsuit, but we will win, Gracie. Mark my words."

Grace relaxed at her father's will. She'd never known her father to lose any battle he set his mind to, and with his support, she would do it. And she wouldn't be alone. "Oh, I know we'll win, Dad."

"Gracie, think about what I said about the Lord. I've wasted six years of my grandson's life. I'd just be sick about it if I didn't know I could make it up in eternity with him."

She flinched. "I'll think about it, Dad, but if there is a God, where's He been?"

"The same place He always was. Where have *you* been? Make an appointment with your lawyer and let me know the day. I'll come down and meet with you, and then I'll finally meet my grandson."

"He looks a lot like you, Dad. He's got your brown eyes and everything."

"I'll talk with your mother before I come down."

"She's not going to come?" Grace bristled. She'd been given back her father. She didn't want her mother in the deal. That would ruin everything.

"No, I think it's best if she stays home this time. I'll be praying about the situation, as I have every day for the past seven years."

"I'll call you soon, Dad."

"Okay, Honey."

Grace pushed the reset button and hung up but let the phone dangle on its cord to the floor. She sank to her knees, crying out at God's relentless pursuit of her. She'd tried to ignore her childhood, ignore that she ever took part in Sunday school or a little childish prayer uttered at seven. But He wouldn't release her. As angry as Grace was at God's people, she couldn't deny she wanted that peace back. Not the legalism or her mother's cold, letter-of-the-law ways, but the comfort she'd once felt when she walked and talked with a heavenly Father daily.

She took several cleansing breaths and knew there was no escaping. If she continued one more day on her own, she was going to crack. She needed help, and God had sought her as His one lost lamb.

"Okay, God, I'm here. My dad says You have been here all along. I suppose that's true in some ways, but I sure have felt alone. I'm sorry You spoke, and I never listened. Surrounding me with Christians at every turn lately was playing a little dirty, but I suppose I needed the wake-up. Please forgive me, Lord. Forgive me, and mark Josh for your kingdom. I'll take him to church every Sunday. I'll let him know all my father taught me, but love him, Lord. Call him to You." Grace looked up at the ceiling. "That's what you've been doing, isn't it? Calling my son to you? Using Fireman Mike, his teacher, the church. You've surrounded my son too. Oh, Lord, now I truly understand what you gave up. I wouldn't part with Josh for anyone's sins, much less my mother's. But You did that. You gave Your Son, who was worthy, for us who aren't. Forgive me, Lord. Forgive me."

Grace sobbed with relief and overwhelming emotion deep

into the night. She'd been welcomed back into two Fathers' arms in one night. And for once, she felt loving arms around her instead of the cold judgment and wrath. Just like when she was a child, before she let anger toward her mother and hypocrites at the church taint her view of God.

Grace sat up, blinking. She would go to church on Sunday with Josh, Fireman Mike, and Miss Jensen. They could play family with someone else's child. She was reclaiming Josh once and for all.

eleven

Mike closed the cover on his Bible and stood tall, stretching out his back. He rubbed his chin, confirming he had, indeed, shaved that morning. Satisfied that he was stubble-free, he moseyed into the kitchen and made himself a bowl of cereal. Usually on Sunday, he was excited to get on with the day, to worship, and be refilled for the week, but today wasn't a normal Sunday. He'd take a child to church this Sunday, a child whose mother feared the Lord's Word.

Grace's salvation weighed heavily on his soul, and he'd spent the morning in prayer for her. He prayed she would change her mind about attending service this morning, and mostly, he prayed God would speak to her. Something just seemed inappropriate about taking Josh and Emily, yet leaving Grace behind.

Dressed in his khaki slacks and tie, he straightened his collar and headed for his truck. What was this pressing emotion he felt about seeing Emily? They'd spent countless days at church together before. Mike worried he'd come to care far too much about Grace Brawlins, and it was affecting his chance for a real romance with a Christian woman. Why couldn't he desire the opportunity to be with Emily? To woo her and take it to the next level? What was it that held him back?

The drive was short and familiar. Arriving at Grace's cottage, he noticed the tulips lining the walkway were in full bloom. An array of color hit his senses, a testimony to her gentle care for the rented home. The house appeared storybook, and Mike marveled that no man was there to appreciate this perfectly-kept home. Grace probably wanted it that way.

Thinking back to his overgrown lawn and unvacuumed carpet, he couldn't help but wish someone took care of him that way—not just as a housekeeper, but as a homemaker—someone who enjoyed making a house nice for the people who lived there. He shook the thought off and started up the walkway. Just as he approached the door, a horn broke his silent reverie.

He turned, and Emily waved. He stopped to wait for her. She scrambled out of the car, then tried to compose herself by smoothing her dress. She wore a straight floral skirt that blew elegantly in the wind. Her shoes, a soft periwinkle blue, matched perfectly. Still, her appearance didn't weaken his knees or his resolve. He prayed for the Lord to lead him— that he wasn't focusing on the impossible while passing the woman Jesus had for him.

"Hi!" Emily said brightly. Her face was carefully made-up with a light shimmer of lip gloss and soft eye shadow to match her eyes. "What impeccable timing, huh?"

"Perfect," Mike said, but something didn't feel perfect. Something felt incredibly awkward. He thought back to the scorched dinner and her angry tantrum. She had a right to be upset. He was spending time with another woman, focusing on another family. Emily deserved better than that. He forced his guilt down. Perhaps it was time to start again.

"I hope Josh is ready. I don't think his mother was too keen on letting us have him for the day." Emily winked as though the two of them had conspired against Grace.

He took a deep breath. He was imagining things. Emily was a kind and sweet woman. She was not conspiring anything. He cleared his throat. "I prayed all morning Grace would join us."

Emily laughed, then covered her mouth with her manicured hand. "I'm sorry. It's just that I don't think Grace Brawlins will ever be interested in church. She has kind of a nasty attitude." Emily crinkled her nose. "But I'm glad you prayed, Mike."

He rang the doorbell, choosing to ignore the comment. Grace opened the door, wearing a smile that caused his heart to pound against his chest. Her blond hair was wrapped up into a barrette on top of her head, and tendrils hung in all the right ways framing her heart-shaped face and flawless skin. Grace's blue eyes met his, and he forgot to speak. There was a softness to her, an innocence she couldn't feign. Her gorgeous lilac suit embraced her figure without being inappropriate, and Mike fell utterly speechless.

"Hey! Well, good morning," Grace finally said. "It's nice to see you both."

"You—you look beautiful." He finally stammered. From the corner of his eye, he could see Emily staring at him, but it wasn't his fault. The words had tumbled out of their own volition. He was lucky he didn't say, *I love you, Grace. I've never seen a woman who set my heart into overdrive like this. Marry me.* He laughed at himself and his uncharacteristic loss of any cool he might possess.

"Yes, you do look nice, Miss Brawlins. Are you planning to do that quiet brunch we discussed?" Emily asked. "I bet if you go early, there won't be anyone in the restaurant."

Grace stood tall. "No, actually, I can't really afford to spend money on something so frivolous right now. I'm planning to come to church with the three of you and see what this is all about. It's been a long time."

Emily's smile faded, and Mike knew it best to refrain from further enthusiastic comments for Emily's sake. "We'd love to have you." He tried to stay monotone, when in actuality he wanted to scream from the rooftops, *This is the perfect woman for me, Lord. If she could only know You. Please, let her know You.* "Where's Josh? Usually, he's bouncing off the walls by now."

"He's drawing the two of you a picture. He said he had to finish it before we leave. Come on in for a minute." Grace stepped back and motioned them in. Her home smelled like fabric softener and lavender-scented candles with a touch of eucalyptus. He inhaled deeply but noted Emily glared at him, and he looked at some of the photographs around to avoid her gaze.

"Your furniture is just beautiful. I meant to comment on it before." Mike smoothed his hand along an elegant mahogany table with a marbled top.

"You've been here before?" Emily questioned.

"Yes, remember when I brought Josh the InCharge CD? You were with me, Emily." He decided to forego the explanation of the day in Monterey out of sheer concern for his life.

"Oh, right," Emily said with a smirk.

Grace motioned for them to sit down. "You won't believe this, but all that furniture was bought at Goodwill and estate sales! I bought it for pennies and refinished it. Josh helped me a lot, and that furniture will last a lifetime now. They just don't make it that way any longer." Grace moved about the room gracefully, clearly proud of the humble abode she'd made into a showplace. "Some people are so careless about what they dispose of, but their loss is my gain." Her eyebrows lifted in her enthusiasm.

"Isn't it kind of gross, going through people's old stuff?" Emily wrinkled her nose.

"Oh, no. Josh and I love it, especially when you can get the history of who it belonged to. It's so much more exciting to have something that tells a story than something off a showroom floor." Grace started to sit, but stood back up. "Can I get you some water or anything? Coffee, Miss Jensen? I know the Boy Scout here doesn't drink it, but you might." Grace giggled, looking away from him, in the most charming display he'd ever seen.

"No, no, thank you. I don't drink it either." Emily's eyes flashed.

"Well, you two will never have to bleach your teeth, and you'll both stay much younger looking. I'll be haggard and visiting the dentist often, but I'll do so happily with my caffeine in hand." Grace held up her forefinger.

Josh came bounding out of the kitchen, trailing two papers behind him. "You're here! You're here!" His enthusiasm was that of a new puppy for its owner.

"We're here." Miss Jensen bent down and reached for her picture. "Who are these wonderful people you drew, Josh?"

"That's my mom and me and Fireman Mike."

"Who's this over here?" Emily traced her finger to the edge of the sheet.

"That's you, Miss Jensen."

Mike sucked in a deep breath. It was going to be a long, uncomfortable morning. "We should get going. Church is about to start."

The four of them drove in edgy silence to church, and Mike found himself locked in prayer for the duration. When they arrived at church, he thought it best to take Josh to Sunday school while the ladies found a seat. Emily readily agreed and carted Grace away toward the sanctuary.

"Josh, are you going to be okay in there?"

"Oh, yeah, Mike." Josh balled up his fists on his wiry hips. "I'll be fine. I told the kids I was coming. They'll be happy to see me."

"Okay, Buddy. We'll see you in about an hour and a half." Mike mussed the child's hair and made sure that all the kids saw him drop Josh off. A few kids enveloped Josh, and they ran off happily.

≈

Grace marveled at the friendliness of the church. Everyone seemed to have a smile on his face, and she found herself thinking maybe something had changed in the Body since she'd been a part of it. People actually looked happy to be there—everyone except Emily Jensen. Grace felt for her. If she dated a man like Mike Kingston, she wouldn't want another woman within one hundred miles of him either. She hoped to put the woman at ease.

"I haven't been to church for years. It's a perfect spring day to start again, don't you think?"

"Uh-huh," Emily said absently.

"Lunch is probably going to be a little long for Josh and me. Maybe you and Mike could drop us off after the service, or we could walk home, and you could have a nice lunch by yourselves."

Emily brightened for the first time that morning. "Yes, I can see where you'll be missing your time with Josh. That's probably a good idea. Mike is leaving for his training tomorrow. It will be a week before I see him again."

"Well, then, you'll definitely want to go without us third wheels. It was sweet of you both to include us this morning. I do appreciate the gesture." Since Grace couldn't think of another thing to say to Josh's teacher, they watched the people gathering after finding a seat on the aisle.

Many people introduced themselves, and Grace was shocked so many recognized her as a visitor. At her parents' church, she usually slipped into the back pew and never heard from a soul. She also noted people were dressed differently. Some wore suits and ties. Some wore nice jeans and button-up shirts. Grace's eyes were probably wide with her shock, and she read her bulletin to keep from staring.

"Josh is all set. He knew quite a few of the kids, and they ran off together." Mike's eyebrows lifted, and Grace could tell he was as pleased as she that Josh found some playmates. Mike sat beside Emily, and she took his hand. Grace looked away, avoiding the jealousy that lurked within. She would not come between a man and his girlfriend. Even though Mike said it was over, Grace would believe it when she saw it. Attending church and lunch together didn't exactly imply they were apart. She settled back into the pew and waited for the music to start.

The music was uplifting and easily transported Grace to tears. She closed her eyes and sang along, feeling the hot tears glide down her cheeks and not caring a bit. It felt as though she had never left the flock. The music washed over her soul like a tonic.

The pastor spoke on the prodigal son, and Grace smiled through her tears. It appeared God had a special message for her, and her alone. After the message, Grace jumped up eagerly. "I'm going to get Josh. Where is he?"

"Grace, wait a minute. Do you want to talk to someone?" Mike asked.

Grace shook her head. "No, I want to go home and talk to Josh. I have a lot to tell him today."

"Are you sure?" Emily's face softened, and she showed legitimate concern.

Grace wanted to share her renewed faith, but this wasn't the time or place. The moment would arrive when Emily and Mike would know, but it wouldn't be today. She had to let her feelings sink in, let the emotions settle into reality before she told anyone.

Mike wanted to ask her. Everything in his face said so, and Grace met his eyes in understanding. *I want to tell you, but I don't want you to think it's a ploy for your affections. Emily is a nice, untainted woman. Make the most of starting fresh. You deserve it.* Grace looked to the floor, away from his sapphire eyes and what they did to her heart. Loneliness had become her continual companion, and she wouldn't play with a man's heart again—especially a man who belonged to another. The man would go on with his life, and she would be alone again. Josh deserved all of her, and that's what she intended to give him.

"Miss Jensen, thank you so much for asking Josh and me today. It means a lot to us." Grace took Emily's hand. "You are very kind, and I appreciate you thinking of us. It's been a long time since Josh and I attended a church. It's such a beautiful day that I think we'll walk home and enjoy it."

"I hope you'll come again." Emily looked her straight in the eye. "And I mean that."

"Mike, can you point me in the right direction for Josh?"

"I'll take you there," Mike looked down on the petite Emily. "You don't mind. Lunch can wait, right?"

"No, no, Mike. I'll find him. Just tell me where." He pointed to an outer building, and Grace nodded. "Have a nice lunch, you two. Thank you. Oh, and Mike, good luck at your training tomorrow."

તે

Mike watched as Grace effortlessly strode toward the Sunday school building. What was it about that woman that attracted his attention so? It wasn't just her beauty. There was an inner sweetness she exuded. In anyone else, he might have thought it was the Holy Spirit pouring out of her, but Grace had told him how she felt about the Lord. He gulped, turning to see Emily staring up at him.

"I think church spoke to her," Emily commented.

"I think so," Mike said. "I prayed it would. I guess we shouldn't be so surprised."

"Did you still want to get lunch?" Emily twisted the toe of her shoe on the patio, and Mike put an arm around her.

"Of course, I do. I'm sorry, Emily. I haven't been a very good friend to you lately. My mind has been occupied with Josh."

"It's all right, Mike. I think we both know this isn't going anywhere. We're friends." Emily shrugged. "That's good, isn't it?"

Mike squeezed his arm about her tighter. "It is good." But the pit of his stomach felt sick. Mike was approaching thirty-four without a serious relationship to his credit. What was wrong with him?

He saw Grace holding hands with Josh, and the two of them smiling gaily. He bit his lip until it nearly bled. He wanted a family. Maybe that's why Grace appealed to him so. She'd already set up housekeeping: a sweet little cottage with flowers up the walk, a warm home with love and a child. All that was missing was a father. How easy it would have been to step into the role.

Mike sighed, forcing the romantic notions down. He needed to get away and think. The training would do him good. He had to get past these thoughts he wrestled with. Grace Brawlins had a complete life without him or the Lord. But how he prayed it would include them both.

"Earth to Mike." Emily waved her hand in front of his face. "You there?"

"Sorry." Mike laughed. "I think I've been off the job too

long. My mind is starting to go. I need to get back to it." He clapped his hands and rubbed them together. "I need a good emergency to spark the old adrenaline."

"You've been off for a few days. Is something the matter?"

"The captain just thinks I've been getting a little too involved lately. He just saw some things. I reacted badly. It's nothing."

"I don't know how you can see some of the things you do on a daily basis and not be affected. You'd be a robot if you weren't." Emily pursed her lips. "Doesn't the captain see that? Emotions are a good thing."

Mike laughed. "Sometimes they are. Sometimes they aren't. Where are we going for lunch?"

"How about the Stratford Hotel? They've got a nice brunch, and we need to celebrate."

"We do? What are we celebrating?"

"We're celebrating that we're friends."

Mike's stomach lurched. "I'm not sure that's something to celebrate."

"Sure it is. Lots of people waste years figuring life out. We only took a few months. That's not bad, and maybe God has our perfect mates waiting out there for us. Maybe He's freeing us up for those special people." Emily laughed.

Mike saw Grace and Josh skip down the walk. Grace unclipped her barrette and let her locks cascade down her back. Mike's pulse quickened. "I sure hope so, Emily, but I'm leery."

"Cautiously optimistic. That sounds better." Emily took his hand, and they walked toward his truck. Grace looked back at them, offering both a smile and a wave.

twelve

Grace had about a week of peace before the warfare started. Every time she answered the phone, she braced herself against a chair, preparing for the barrage of words each call might bring. Lawyers, witnesses, friends; some offering support, some threatening her with slander.

It never occurred to her that the battle might come to her front door as well. Saturday morning began as any other. Grace cleaned and folded laundry while Josh played with his building set and Batman figurines. The doorbell rang.

"I'll get it!" Josh raced to answer the door, nearly knocking Grace over in the process. He swung it open and stepped back, his face puzzled. "Mom?"

Grace's mouth went dry. Josh's father filled the doorway, still handsome as ever. She used the back of the sofa to maintain her upright position. She felt faint when those dark, elusive eyes stared into hers.

He hadn't seen her yet, and it gave her a moment to compose herself. "Is your mom home?" He stared at Josh in a way that made Grace uncomfortable. . .as if he was trying to see any resemblance that might satisfy his sick curiosity.

"I'm here, Lyle." Grace stood tall, forcing her shoulders back. How hard it was to believe this weak-willed, dangerous man was Josh's father! Josh deserved so much better. What had she ever seen behind those dark eyes? Had she lost all discernment?

"Josh, you should get dressed. Fireman Mike will be home

from his training by now and is on his way to get you for the zoo."

"Yes!" Josh pulled his upturned fist and bent elbow toward him. Then, he ran toward his bedroom, not giving Lyle Covington a second glance.

"I really wish you wouldn't come here again. Josh is very impressionable, and I'd like him kept ignorant of this situation."

Lyle disregarded her comment and stepped into the home, uninvited. Sitting on the couch and sprawling his arms out over the sofa's full back, he propped an expensively clad foot over his knee. "If you want me to pay for him, he's going to have to know *you* think I'm his daddy. You can't have it both ways, Gracie."

"You are not his daddy. You are his birth father, and you have a legal obligation to pay for him. The law says so." Grace lowered her voice. "Don't think that gives you any parental rights to him. If you really wanted to be a father to him, that would be one thing, but you just want to hurt me."

"Grace." He looked down, shaking his head. "Grace, I can just deny I ever knew about him." He shrugged, pressing his lips together. "Then I could request time with my son. . . maybe even custody?" One of his eyebrows lifted. He looked around the cottage. "I'm certainly in a better financial position to take the boy."

Grace laughed and crossed her arms. She remained standing. "Don't you dare threaten me. I'll only use it against you in court. Your discovery people aren't doing nearly the job they once did." She paced, feeling as though she was the prosecutor in trial, catching her guilty party in a web of lies. "Maybe your father should never have fired me. I wouldn't let something so big slip through the cracks." She clicked her tongue. "Sloppy, sloppy."

"Pardon me?" Lyle's dark eyes peered at her, as though he couldn't be trifled with.

Grace nearly burst into laughter. Once, she might have been so fearful of that look, but after raising a son by herself, she had nothing left to fear. Certainly not this weak man who hid behind his wallet and credentials.

"The check." Grace let one corner of her lips curve. "You wrote me a check, and the date on it just happens to coincide with the three month mark of my pregnancy. Not only that, but you enclosed a note telling me what to do with that check. And here I thought it was for baby clothes."

She watched him swallow, and his jaw set. "All right. What do you want?"

"I want child support, just like the complaint says. I'm not going after back support, though I should." Grace checked to make sure Josh's door was shut. "You have a wonderful little boy in there, who thankfully, is nothing like you." She pointed at him. "Would you let your own child live hand-to-mouth any longer while you marry some society girl? While you travel around the world? Drive a fancy sports car? It's not right, Lyle."

"You never cashed that check," he said, obviously hoping to find out if she was bluffing. "There's no record of it. I checked." Again, a smug smile emerged.

"No, I never cashed it; but luckily, I did save it. I'm very sentimental that way, Lyle. In case you ever tried to come back in my life, I wanted to remember what you wished for your own child." Grace closed her eyes, shoving such evil thoughts away. *Praise God, Josh was safe.*

"I don't want to go to court with this mess. It will be public, and it will ruin my fiancée's wedding day." He crossed his arms. "Tell me what you want."

She looked at the contempt in his eyes. Lyle obviously blamed her completely for his having to complicate his neat little life with such ugly details. "I want a monthly settlement to cover private school for Josh, and a college scholarship fund started that will mature when he's eighteen. I'll manage clothes and food on my own."

"Why private school? You live in one of the finest neighborhoods in California."

"I want Josh in Christian school from here on out. I have my reasons." Grace could list them extensively, but she didn't. She'd led Josh so astray. She wanted to start making up for lost time, and she felt Christian school was just one way to help ease the burden. At least he'd be with people who loved children, rather than teenagers just trying to earn a buck after school.

"You'll keep this out of court if you get your money?"

"That money won't begin to harm your lifestyle or take anything away from your children when you decide to have them. I think it's fair, and it will give Josh the head start he needs."

"Fine." His jaw twitched. "Have your lawyer turn your requests in to my lawyer. I'll have something drawn up."

"*I'll* have something drawn up. I know the way your firm does business, remember?" Grace lifted a brow. "And remember, I'm far better at discovery than anyone you've got working there. Your father is far too cheap with his paralegals. When will you see how that costs you?"

"Why now, Grace? Why did you decide to come after me now? You've had plenty of time to make a case if you wanted money. Why ruin my wedding?"

"You think that's what this is about, don't you? Me ruining your life? Did you ever stop to think how you've harmed your son's life? How your playing around created a child? Not an inconvenience for your wedding date, but a real, living, precious child?"

"Spare me the right-to-life garbage, okay? Why now?"

"I've made a lot of mistakes in my life, Lyle." Grace sat down on the chair beside him, and clasped her hands together. "I forgive you for your part in all this. I'm actually grateful to you for Josh. But how could I deny him what's rightfully his? He is already missing a father in his life; he shouldn't be continuously living in want too."

"If you forgive me, why the lawsuit? Don't you know my firm is famous for such cases?"

"I filed the lawsuit before things changed in my life. I wouldn't have filed it today, though I still would have gone after the money. It's about consequences, Lyle. It's not right that the government should pay in grants for Josh to attend college, when you easily could write a check for what your son needs." Grace drew in a breath. "I'm giving you the chance to do things right. Look at it that way. He deserves better than I can provide for him by myself."

"You're not going to come after me when I get settled with my bride, now are you?"

Grace shook her head. "It's not about revenge. Maybe it started that way, Lyle, but it's about doing what's right. I won't interfere with your marriage. I'll even have it written in the agreement to show you. I hope you'll have a good life with her. Honestly. But you made a child. Regardless of what you wanted to happen, Josh happened."

"Okay, Grace." He slapped his thighs and rose from the couch. "You win. Send your agreement to the firm."

Josh came bounding out the door. "I got my InCharge shorts on, Mom. Fireman Mike is going to think they are so cool."

Lyle watched his son and blinked several times. "In-Charge, huh?"

"Yeah, they rock." Josh broke into a dance step, and Lyle snickered.

"He's a nice kid, Grace." Lyle left, and Grace watched through the window as he drove off in a pristine SUV. She heaved a deep breath and muttered a silent prayer. That was far better than she'd imagined. Perhaps she could trust in God again.

Fireman Mike swerved out of Lyle's way to get into the driveway. Looking back at the expensive car, Mike appeared melancholy. Grace's heart pounded at the sight of his familiar truck. She'd missed him so.

He got out, smiling. After seeing Lyle's slight frame, Mike looked muscular and unimaginably tall. Grace could make out the sapphire color in his eyes from where she stood, and her stomach flip-flopped. Josh ran past her toward him, and Mike lifted him in the air and spun him before setting him back down.

"Check out those shorts, Dude!" Mike slowly nodded in approval.

"Mom got them for me. Aren't they the best?"

"Just like your mom." Mike winked at her, and she looked away.

Her breath caught, and she pretended to sneeze to avoid being so moved by his simple gesture. She stepped out onto the walkway, relishing her giant tulips and the wash of color they provided. She concentrated on the pinks and yellows rather than dwell where she really wanted to focus.

"How was your hazard training?"

He came beside her, lightly touching her shoulder. "Are you talking to me or that tulip there?"

She turned to face him, but her stomach twisted and swirled, so she bent and rearranged the self-watering apparatus. "I was talking to you. The flowers don't usually answer." She nibbled nervously on her lip. Why couldn't she maintain her composure around this gorgeous wall of a man? Was she so shallow that she could be so easily affected by an incredible exterior?

"The training was good. Trying. I hope I'll never have to deal with such an emergency, but I'm prepared now. I just need to train the rest of the force, now that I'm back. Apparently, I'm the only one with an attention span long enough to withstand those cerebral training sessions, so they always send me." He caught a ball Josh threw at him. "I can read anything. A mind like a trap, my mom used to say." He laughed. "Well, you can buy all the intellectual excuses, or you can figure I'm single, and no one else wanted to go."

Grace checked her watch and stood. "So, what are you boys up to today?"

"The zoo. Josh says his monkey friends miss him."

Josh jumped at Mike, and they pretended to fight. "They're your friends!"

Grace laughed at her son's attempt at humor. "Well, I hope you both plan to visit the hippos because they take baths!"

"Mom!"

"Join us." Mike's smile disappeared, and he zeroed in on her eyes, unwilling to let her gaze go.

"I have laundry to do, the grass to mow, and groceries to buy. You guys have a great time." She thought about Emily Jensen and what she might think of the invitation, and guilt enveloped her. Emily was her son's teacher, and Grace knew what it felt like to be played like an instrument. She wouldn't succumb to Mike's natural charms. She needed to find herself, to get grounded in the Lord. She wasn't ready for any commitments until she knew her faith was solid again.

Mike was not so easily deterred. "The laundry can wait. I'll take you out to dinner, and the lawn will wait until next weekend when Josh and I can mow it."

"This is Josh's special time with you. I wouldn't want to—"

"Grace, it's been a week since I've seen you." He clutched the ball Josh threw at him. "A week since I've seen Josh," he corrected. "Josh only gets so much time with you. Come with us, unless you need the break."

Grace looked at him from the corner of her eyes. "When you say dinner, are you talking Big Mac?"

He laughed. "No, I think I could spring for a Whopper."

"Oh my, but you are a big spender."

"I'd treat you to lobster, but I have a feeling Josh would protest. How about Chili's?"

"Hmm," Grace pressed a finger to her chin, tapping it. "Chili's. You sure know how to woo a girl."

"Hey, some women appreciate a fine wine; you appreciate a restaurant with spill-proof drink cups."

Grace laughed. "Well, since I'm up against Bond himself, I guess I better agree. I am powerless to resist spill-proof cups." Grace shook her head and clicked her tongue. "I should have known you'd find the chink in my armor."

"Yes!" Josh's face crinkled, showing his missing front teeth.

"What about Emily? Will she be joining us?" Grace felt the need to remind him of his girlfriend. Grace didn't want to be known as a temptress, and yet it felt so wonderful to play family with Josh and Mike.

Mike sighed. "No, Emily and I have decided to concentrate on friendship." He tossed the sponge football toward Josh. "I hope that won't stop you from joining us at church tomorrow."

"Mom said we're going to go to church from now on, Mike! I can't wait to tell the kids."

Mike raised his eyebrows. "What's this about?"

"We'll talk about it later. I'm going to run and get my windbreaker. Sometimes, it gets awfully cold in the city, even in the summer." Grace scrambled into the house, nearly hyperventilating. He was free. She fell into prayer as naturally as when she was a child.

Oh, Lord, You are enough, so why am I so tempted by this man of flesh and bones? I am not a good judge of character, Lord. You know that. I thought Lyle was sweet, caring, and considerate at one time too. Remember? Today, Lyle didn't flinch at the sight of his own son. I want to believe Michael Kingston is different, that he is a true man of faith, but that's exactly why I cannot believe it. I must focus on You, and what You can provide—not on a man. No man can take away my troubles and heal us, Lord. Only You.

Grace opened her eyes and went to the door. Mike and Josh were in the kitchen, fumbling about with things, and she followed the noise. "What's going on in here?"

"We're packing a picnic lunch, Mom. Mike said you'd like that. He said the zoo had lots of nice places to picnic." Josh dragged a chair to the sink to wash an apple.

"I'll get the cooler." Grace scrambled out of the kitchen. She just wasn't ready to deal with all the emotions Mike made her feel.

ᕍ

Mike watched Josh wash the apples, then dry them on his T-shirt. Tossing a towel his way, Mike raised an eyebrow, and Josh washed the apples again using the towel this time.

"So, how were you this week, Bud? Did you take good care of your mom?"

"Yeah. She was kinda sad this week, though. Whenever I saw her, she was crying all the time. She told me it was happy tears, but she didn't look too happy to me."

Mike thought a moment, but his curiosity was getting the best of him. "Why did your Mom say you could go to church now?"

Josh shrugged. "Don't know. She just said we were going from now on, and I was going to meet my grandpa soon."

"Your grandpa?"

"Yeah. I thought he was in heaven, but Mom said he was in Modesto, not heaven. I hope that means I'll get to meet my dad soon too."

Mike stopped making the sandwiches and focused on Josh. "You've never met your father?"

Josh shook his head.

"My dad left my mom and me too." Mike thought to himself, *How could anyone make such a choice?*

"Mom said he went away before I was born. She said that was okay because he wasn't very smart, or he wouldn't have left in the first place."

Mike forced back a laugh. "Your mom is right about that. I can't imagine having a better son than you, Josh."

"That's good. Because I been thinking you should be my dad." Josh placed the apples in a big paper bag and looked at him with wide eyes.

Mike took Josh's chin in his hands. "It's not that simple, Buddy. I wish it were, but it's not. Maybe your mom will get married someday, and you'll have a stepfather; but until then, I think we should keep spending time together."

Josh shook his head. "I don't want a stepfather. I want a real father. Mom would pick someone boring. Someone who wore a suit everyday. Besides, she's not interested."

Mike thought about the nice-looking man who left the house in a costly SUV. Had *that man* been interviewing for the position? Dining the elegant Grace Brawlins while he was away? Mike already decided the man's car was far too expensive to let a little kid eat McDonald's in it. He hoped Grace realized that.

"She's not interested in what, Buddy?"

"In getting married." Josh shrugged. "That's why I gotta find my own daddy."

"Josh." Mike sat beside the boy on a barstool. "You can't just make somebody your daddy. I wish you could, but you can't. Your mom gets to choose that."

"But she did already, and she said my daddy wasn't smart enough to stay. That's why I want you to change her mind about marrying, and marry her. Or she might pick someone stupid again."

Mike laughed aloud. "What makes you think I have the ability to do that?"

"You told me with God, all things can happen. I prayed, and things are gonna happen. But you have to help. You already got her to agree to church. That's something."

The hope in Josh's eyes was something Mike couldn't bear to dash. He remembered those feelings like they were yesterday—yearning for someone to play ball with and teach him to ride a bike. Watching the other kids in the neighborhood run to their daddies after a long day's work. He prayed for strength. He had to show Josh that he would be there as much as possible but also that Grace Brawlins was another matter altogether.

"My dad left, and I never got another father, other than my heavenly One, Josh. Maybe you won't either, but that doesn't mean—"

Josh shook his head wildly. "My mom's prettier than Miss Jensen."

Mike looked away, unwilling to answer such charges.

"She probably cooks better too."

"Josh, there are things you are just too young to understand. Two people must love each other to be married, but they also must love the Lord together for it to work." Mike stopped at the sight of Grace in the doorway. His eyes widened. "I'm sorry, Grace. I know how you feel about my discussing religion with Josh, but—"

She held up a hand. "I think marriage is a discussion I should have with my son, Mike. It's personal, and I will handle it."

"The same way you handle religion?"

Grace's eyes narrowed. "Joshua, please go to your room."

"But—"

"Go!"

Josh scrambled from sight. A slamming door echoed a moment later.

"Michael Kingston, I do appreciate what you've done for my son. I don't know how I could live with myself if I thought of him in daycare all day without your occasional visit. Don't think me ungrateful, but you're going to get married someday soon, and no woman is going to share you with Josh. That's just a fact of life. I will be left to pick up the pieces, so please don't lecture me on life lessons. I've more than earned my stripes."

"Grace." He stepped closer. "Why church? Why now?" He prayed it was because of him, that he had sparked something within her that made her yearn for the Holy Spirit.

She turned around, busying her hands with the cooler. He grasped them between his own. Her hands were soft and slender as though they'd never done a day's work, but he knew how ridiculous that was.

"I can't answer that. Not yet."

He looked down at her blue eyes. One of them held a tear. He caressed her face with his hand. "Please tell me, Grace." His heart pounded, and he prayed she'd tell him she'd entered into a relationship with Jesus, but she only blinked away her tears. "Grace?"

She snuggled against him, the warmth of her cheek against his racing heart. Her hair smelled of botanicals, and Mike combed his fingers through her hair, tangling them in her ponytail. He kissed the top of her head, and they held each other for a long time. How long he didn't know, but it felt like mere seconds. Josh opened his door, and the two of them quickly separated.

thirteen

It had been years since Grace had visited the zoo. She could hear the distant waves of the Pacific Ocean and feel the bite of the morning fog, but the sun peeked through the cypress trees, promising a brilliant day in San Francisco. It was early yet, and the crowds hadn't gathered. Josh ran ahead down the hill toward the hippos and big cats. Grace flushed red at the sight of her overly enthusiastic son.

"I don't get to do much of this kind of thing with him."

"Grace, you don't have to apologize. That's why I wanted to help, so Josh could do more of this kind of thing." Mike started to reach for her hand, but she pointed toward the lions, frustrating his effort. She saw the hurt in his eyes, and she wished she could tell him everything—how she'd given her life back to God. But her father would be in town soon. She wouldn't have him thinking Mike was like Lyle. If Mike was the right man for her, he would be there when her father left town.

"I'm glad you're helping us. It's made a world of difference to Josh. And me. You reminded me of some very important truths in this life."

"He says he'll be meeting his grandpa. Is that true?"

Grace nodded. "I called him to tell him about the lawsuit." She sucked in a quick breath, covering her mouth.

"The lawsuit?"

"I'm filing against Josh's father for child support." Grace watched as Mike's expression melted into a frown. "Well, actually I think we reached a settlement."

"His father?" Mike crossed his arms behind his back. "I guess I never thought about the fact that there was a father." He laughed a forced, confused laugh. "I can be pretty naïve sometimes. I just assumed he was out of the picture completely, like my own father was." He looked at Josh, and then back to her, his expression pained.

"He is." Grace searched his face. "Lyle is out of the picture. He's getting married next month."

"Has Josh met him?"

"Today. That was him at the house, driving away when you came."

"I see."

"Mike, it's not what you're thinking."

Mike clicked his tongue. "I'm not thinking anything. It's none of my business." He shrugged. "Josh is pretty enamored with that lion over there. I think I'll go talk with him about it."

Grace sucked in a deep breath as she watched Mike's muscular frame as he walked away. She thought he'd be happy for them—happy that Josh's father would finally provide the much-needed financial support. But that's how people were, saying they'd forgive you when your sin was never far from their mind. A lion roared, waking her from her reverie.

Grace studied Mike. He'd lifted Josh up for a better view of an ostrich. Suddenly, her stomach swirled. Would Josh ever have a man who loved him like Mike? Was Mike interested in a woman with a past like hers? Loving her son was one thing, loving the mother who bore him illegitimately, quite another.

She followed Mike, touching him lightly on the shoulder. "I'm using the money from Lyle to send Josh to a private Christian school. I got him entry into Calvary Academy, beginning in the fall."

Mike's eyes softened into a smile. "I'm so glad, Grace. Relieved, actually. Josh will flourish in that environment."

"The kids at Los Altos have been so unkind to him. I want him to be at a place where they appreciate and love him."

"Is that all?"

Grace focused on the lion behind the big, plate glass window. "Should there be more?"

"I just thought maybe, well, you know, the faith was a part of your decision."

Grace looked away from him.

"Most teachers love their kids. Emily certainly loves Josh."

Grace shook her head. "No, I don't think Emily does love Josh. I think she tolerates him because of you, but she doesn't see what's special about him. If she did, she wouldn't punish him for not fitting in or snub her nose at his out-of-style clothes."

"Grace, I can't believe that's true. Emily is a Christian."

"Mike, I mean you no ill will in this, but I've found that makes very little difference in the way some people act. I believe the Bible calls them a clanging gong."

He looked at his shoes. "The world is full of hypocrites, Grace. They are not just in the church."

"You're right, and I'm sorry if I offended you. You've never been a clanging gong to us, Mike. I know Emily means a lot to you, and I shouldn't have shared my opinion, harsh as it is. I need to learn to bite my tongue."

"No, no. If that's what you think, I'm in no position to judge. If you say Emily hasn't been that kind to Josh, I can't argue with you. You would know better."

"Someday, you'll be a father and understand. You'll know what it does to your soul when someone hurts your child— whether or not they meant to. Something just clicks in you."

His cheek flinched, and he crossed his arms. "So I suppose Josh will be seeing his father now."

She grabbed his arm, forcing his eyes to hers. "No. He doesn't want anything to do with Josh."

"How do you know that?"

"He's getting married to a high-society real estate agent. He doesn't have time for an unwanted kid in his life. The money is about fairness, Mike. I just don't want Josh to suffer while Lyle lives the stately life. That's all."

"Grace." He reached for her, cupping his hands around her cheeks. "Josh is not suffering. Not getting the latest InCharge CD is hardly suffering."

"Maybe not, but he's already without a father. I won't make it any more difficult than it has to be."

"So, will this make things simpler? The money?"

"Are you saying I shouldn't be going after child support?"

"Of course not. I don't know what I'm saying. I'm hardly the man to offer you advice, Grace." He dropped his hands to his side. "Forget I said anything."

"Cool, let's go see the zebra!" Josh pulled them both by the hands, forcing an end to their conversation.

❧

Mike's mind wandered as Josh talked to him about the zebra. The child had a bevy of facts from an animal television show, and he relayed them endlessly. Grace seemed preoccupied as well, and he wished he hadn't pressed the subject. Why should it bother him if Grace went after child support? It was rightfully hers for bringing up Josh. He had no reason to deny her the proper support to raise her son. So why did it feel like a vise grip on his heart? He hated the fact that she asked another man for help, that Grace should be indebted to this Lyle character for the gift of Josh.

"Grace, I want us to go out to dinner." He looked around, unsure if he'd actually said the words aloud.

"Sure." Grace shrugged as though nothing was out of the ordinary. "When is your next day off? Josh—"

"No, not Josh. You and me. I want *us* to go out to dinner."

"Why?" Her soft gray-blue eyes clouded.

"I just want to finish a conversation with you. I don't know why." But he did know why. Something about her held his heart and wouldn't let go.

"I don't really have any type of babysitter, and—"

"Grace, do you feel at all what I do?" He held his hands out toward her, trying to stress his point, but not sure if she understood a word he said.

"I don't know if I feel anything, Mike. I'm a little numb."

"Do you," he halted, trying to find the words. *Do you feel this connection, this undeniable attraction for me? Or is it just me?* "Do you want to know me any better?"

"Of course, I do. I can't tell you the stress relief I have felt just in having you care for Josh. Having someone else think he's as special as I do has meant the world to me." She smiled, an innocent sweet grin that told him nothing.

"Never mind."

"Yes! Yes, I want to know you better, Mike. I feel drawn to you. I thought it was the Lord at first. He has called me back to the flock, but it's not just that." She shook her head.

Mike felt as if he'd been struck in the stomach. He clutched it to force the queasiness away, checking the facts to make sure he'd heard correctly. "You are a Christian." He let out a deep sigh. "I thought I felt the Holy Spirit, but I thought it was my own desires, not reality." His fingers raked through his hair.

"It's reality, but it doesn't erase my past reality. My mistakes will always be readily obvious to anyone who cares to check."

Josh ran toward the giraffes. Mike turned to see a man taking pictures of them. At first, he thought it was the animals, but he noticed the man followed them. "Do you know that man, Grace?" Mike pointed, and the man turned. Mike sprinted toward him, and while the man began to run, Mike easily overtook him. He pulled the stranger around by the shoulder. "Who are you?"

The man cowered behind his raised arm. "Don't hurt me."

"I'm not going to hurt you. I rescue people. I don't harm people. Why are you taking photos of us?"

"I was taking a picture of the zebra. You just got in the way." The man was slight in stature, with dark brown eyes, and a receding hairline.

"Did Josh's father send you?"

The man's brows furrowed. "Who?"

"Give me your business card."

"What?" The man shrugged. "I don't have a business card. I'm just taking pictures. Are you paranoid, Man?"

Mike took out his billfold, flashing his badge. "I'm a firefighter. Who are you?"

Standing to his full stature, the little man balked. "I told you, I'm just a guy taking pictures."

Mike crossed his arms in front of him. "You will give me your business card, or I'll take you to the zoo offices, myself, and call the police. You were tailing us, and I want to know why. I've got a lot of friends on the force, and I think they're inclined to believe me if I say you're harassing me. I'm not inclined to lie."

"I'm not going anywhere with you. Leave me be." The photographer stood up straight, dusting off his black polyester pants.

"You see that kid there?"

"Yeah, he your son?"

"Can't you tell me?" Mike scrutinized his face.

"Listen, Buddy, I'm not looking for any trouble." The man reached into his pocket and pulled out a card. "You just leave things be, and I'll do the same, okay?"

Mike scanned the card. *Gilbert Howard, Private Investigator*. "Who are you working for?"

"Listen, you got what you wanted. Let it go. I'm off the case, I promise." The man stuffed his camera into a case, and turned to run. Mike watched him go.

"Mike, who was that?" Grace's eyes held fear. "Why did he want pictures of us?"

"He's no one. Don't worry, Grace. Everything's fine." But in his mind, he watched the slight man scamper into the distance, wondering what this Lyle character might be up to. He ground his teeth together. He wouldn't let anyone harm Grace or Josh.

"I'm sure we're just overreacting. We've been watching too many movies." Grace smiled and took Josh's hand.

Mike turned around and looked behind them again. Paranoid or not, he wasn't about to let another picture be snapped without knowing who wanted them photographed.

fourteen

A few months later

Monday morning greeted Grace like a new friend. The sun shone, and the rolling California hills began to turn from spring's rich green to their calming golden tone of summer. June was upon them. Grace stopped in the entry to her office building and listened to the trickling water of the natural fountain. Lush greenery over mossy rocks soothed her soul. Her mind drifted to Mike, their times together, and the way he showed such warmth for her and Josh.

She wondered if Mike would hold that same warm expression for her alone, though she'd never had the chance to find out. Their plans for that intimate dinner had come and gone several times. She flushed and turned her face up to the heat of the sun. Something always came up, and Josh always seemed to tag along. Would Mike and she ever get time to explore their feelings for one another?

Grace sniffed. *I suppose that's why romance should come before children.* She checked her watch. The fifteenth had finally arrived. Her father would come today, and the very thought sent her heart aflutter. How she missed him in her life! She prayed he would still be the same, that the years would not have taken their toll, and they might not have missed much. Thinking of Josh's years, she knew that simply wasn't possible.

"Miss Brawlins?" A few high-heel clicks on the cement

140

alerted Grace to the tall blond. She looked familiar, but Grace couldn't place her.

"Do I know you?" Grace finally asked.

"I'm Lily Hampton. I'm Lyle's fiancée." The blond hitched her chin to the sky as though her statement was something to be proud of.

Grace wanted to answer, *And I'm the mother of his child. What can I do for you?* She stifled a giggle, and answered more appropriately. "Can I help you? Did you want to sell me a house or something?"

"I hardly find this meeting funny, Miss Brawlins."

"I didn't know this was a meeting." Grace shrugged. "I'm just going to work. What you're doing here is beyond me." Grace flipped her hair in an exaggerated manner. "Usually, when there's a meeting, both parties are made aware of it—just a little tip between us girls."

"Listen. I didn't come here to have your trashy ways give me lessons in manners."

Grace stepped back, shocked anyone would behave so irrationally. "Quite frankly, I don't care what you came here for. If you have something to say to me, tell it to Lyle's lawyer. I'm sure I'll get the message." Grace turned and walked toward her office, but the woman followed her. Grace could hear the hollow clicks of the heels.

"Wait a minute. Wait a minute. I'm sorry. I didn't mean anything by that."

"You didn't mean I was trashy, or that you needed a lesson in manners? Because I'm thinking you do."

"Miss Brawlins, I just need to know something about Lyle. This is personal, and it's not anything a lawyer could answer."

Grace stopped in her tracks, studying the woman. Her confidence had clearly waned from the sophisticated engagement photo Grace had first seen. She looked a bit browbeaten and confused. "Miss Hampton, I haven't seen Lyle but once in seven years, so I'm sure I'm not the one to ask."

"He says this isn't his child, but that he's paying you off because you want so little. Is that true?" Lily Hampton's eyes narrowed. She obviously hoped for an answer Grace couldn't give her.

"He's your husband-to-be. I suppose his answer is your truth, but I'm no charity case, Miss Hampton. I was in law school when my son was born. I would have been a good lawyer, but I'm an excellent paralegal, instead."

"Listen, you don't look anything like I thought you would. You look younger, more innocent. I thought—"

Grace felt her expression soften. "I'm sure whatever Lyle says, he wants to protect you."

"Grace." Mr. Falk's steady, familiar voice broke her train of thought.

"Mr. Falk. Good morning." She heard her voice shake at the sight of her boss.

"I'd like to see you in my office immediately."

Grace nodded. "Of course, Sir." Grace looked back at the professional blond in front of her. The voluptuous figure made Grace feel lanky and childlike. Yet she wouldn't trade places with the woman for anything. For all Grace's faults, her mistake had taught her well. Men like Lyle Covington weren't worth their trouble.

"You have to go," Lily said.

"Yes, I do." Grace studied the red, claw-like nails. *Just like I imagined*, she thought to herself. "Lily, I have no intention of ruining your future. I only want what is rightfully Joshua's."

"You should have taken the check." Lily clicked her tongue and turned, but looked over her shoulder. "There's no reason

Lyle should have to pay for the rest of his life because you couldn't take responsibility for yourself."

Grace felt the blood drain from her face, and she felt light-headed with horror. How could anyone contain such evil behind a carefully designed, glamorous façade?

"We made a child." Grace crossed her arms, thankful her boss had reentered the office. "I don't kill my young. You're perfect for Lyle." Grace called after her. "Good luck. You'll need it." Grace stormed off to her office, holding back the tears she wanted to cry out of sheer anger. She breathed in deeply, the solitary trickle of the waterfall offering no peace whatsoever.

"I'm sorry, Mr. Falk. What did you need?" Grace braced herself against the doorjamb.

"There's a Michael Kingston on the phone. He says it's important."

Grace raced to the phone, clutching it tightly. "Mike?"

"Grace, first, it's nothing to worry about so calm down." His answer caused her to release her breath. "It's actually good news."

"Oh, Mike, I could use some good news about now."

"You know, the photographer who was taking our picture a couple months back?"

"At the zoo. Sure. He really was filming us."

"Turns out, he was."

"Why? Did Lyle put him up to it?"

"No, actually, Lyle had nothing to do with it. He was following me, not you. Shortly before I met you, or right around the time, I'm not sure, I saved a man after he had a heart attack in the grocery store."

"Oh, Mike, that's wonderful!"

"The photographer," Mike continued, "was hired by Travis

Mann, the guy whose life I saved."

"Travis Mann, the computer guy?"

"Yes. He was apparently checking into my background to see if I was the type who might extort money from him."

"How sad. Why would anyone be so suspicious?"

"Unfortunately, I guess he has reason to be. I went to visit him in the hospital. I think that was a mistake. Anyway, he decided I was honest."

"So how did you find out who the photographer was?"

"Mr. Mann called the station house last night. I guess he was checking on my background before he did anything to repay me. I was just doing my job, so of course, I wouldn't accept a personal gift anyway."

"So what's the good news? You're keeping me in suspense."

"Well, Mr. Mann has donated five thousand dollars in new toys for the Christmas toy drive."

"It's June."

Mike chuckled. "Yes, but we collect toys all year round."

"That's wonderful, Mike. Just wonderful."

"He also bought us a new Jaws of Life. Our old tool was seventy-four pounds, and it's seen better days. Our new one is on the way. It's only forty pounds."

"You are full of good news today."

"Wait, here's the part where you come in. Mr. Mann also gave me and each of the guys an expensive gift certificate for a fancy restaurant."

"Wow, he's one grateful guy."

"So I thought we'd use my gift certificate together. I thought you could tell me which fork to use—you know, add a little class to my appearance."

Grace's stomach turned over. Was this the real date she'd dreamed of? She was afraid to ask. She closed her eyes and blurted, "What about Josh?"

"Emily said she'd watch him. We could go on Saturday night."

Grace felt the hair on the back of her neck rise. "I don't think so." Then another, more painful thought drifted into her head. "So you're still seeing Emily?"

"Grace." Mike laughed. "Of course I'm not seeing Emily." He cleared his throat. "I thought I was seeing you. But I'd like to spend a little time together—just the two of us."

Grace wanted nothing more, and at the same time the thought scared her to death. What if Mike and Grace had nothing to say to one another when they were alone? What if Mike and Grace had to be Mike, Josh, and Grace to work?

"My father is coming into town tonight," she announced.

"Grace?"

"I really need to get back to work. Mr. Falk has been more than patient with me this morning."

"There are guys at the station house with families, Grace. I'm sure they'd love to have Josh over for the evening, and he would have friends to play with. I know the guys are all CPR certified and good parents to boot. Please don't say no. You're making me think it's me, not Josh, who's the issue."

Grace looked at her desktop. It was covered with briefs and legal documents. She gnawed at her lip, hesitating in her answer. "Mike, it's not Josh. I know all your friends would be wonderful to him."

"Then it's me."

How could she tell him she wanted to spend time with him like nothing else but feared that would lead them closer to the end. She searched for words, but feared incriminating herself. The Christian community would react to such a handsome, eligible bachelor dating a single mother. Mike could have any beautiful, baggage-free woman he wanted, and maybe that was what Grace feared. Did she care enough to set him free?

"I have to be careful with Lyle checking into everything."

"Lyle can't expect you to have no social life, Grace. You've been on your own for nearly seven years. I think a dinner out is warranted."

"My son's reputation depends on how I behave, Mike. I just don't think it's a good idea to be seen alone together. Not yet, anyway." She bit her lip. It was a lie, and she knew it. Guilt trickled over her.

"Fine." Mike swallowed so she could hear it. "I guess I understand. These months were about Josh."

"Mike?" She heard a soft click. It was too late.

Grace bowed her head in anguish. *I can't toy with him like a kitten's ball of yarn. If it ends after the dinner, it ends, but I can't lie to him. What's wrong with me?*

"Grace? I need you in this meeting." Mr. Falk stood at the doorway. Grace looked to the phone. Her apology would have to wait.

❧

"What's the matter, Buddy?" Jared patted Mike on the back. "We're going to the grocery store. You about ready?"

"What is wrong with me, Jared? Do I have sap written on me somewhere?" Mike traced a finger over his forehead.

"What are you talking about?"

"I asked Grace to dinner with my certificate, but she doesn't want to be seen with me. I think she's probably just waiting to see if her son's father comes back to them." Mike slammed the phone in the cradle again for emphasis. "It's just like all the women around here. They all want someone with a billfold. A firefighter can't give them that kind of lifestyle. Not even with the occasional gift certificate," he snorted.

Jared sat on a weight bench, crossing his legs at the ankles. "That sounds a bit harsh, don't you think? Grace has given up a lot to raise her son right. You told me so, yourself. That doesn't sound like the kind of woman who's after a billfold. Besides, you two have spent a lot of time together. You just getting wind of this now?"

"You know, when she became a Christian, I just assumed that she was who God had for me. That's why I had been given a heart for Josh. It all made sense to me, but anytime I try to move it forward a bit, into another realm, you might say, she puts the brakes on me." Mike dipped his head. "I've had enough of this. I'm single. I'm going to stay that way. Women just make you crazy—especially when they look like Grace Brawlins."

Jared laughed. "Yeah, they do. As a married man of ten years, I can testify they definitely make you crazy. But I wouldn't trade mine for anything in this world."

Mike sighed. And wasn't it the truth? "So what now?"

"Now, you pray. You pray and you wait. You did that with Emily, right?"

Mike's eyebrows raised, "Um, yeah. . .and look how that turned out."

"Yeah, let's do. You found out that Emily Jensen goes to church every Sunday, but doesn't really live out her faith. You found out that she was sweet to a fatherless little boy in front of you, but cruel when you weren't around. Is that the kind of woman you would have wanted for life?"

"Well, no, but—"

"But nothing, Mike. Anything worth having is worth fighting for. And especially praying for. When you go into a burning building because you know someone might be in it, why do you do it?"

Mike laughed. "That's a dumb question. Because some-one's life might be at stake."

"And yet you put your life on the line, not really knowing if there's another life at stake or not. You go in on faith and experience."

"What's your point?"

"Part of being ready for marriage is God preparing your heart. If you're ready to toss Grace aside so easily, maybe you're not ready for the commitment of marriage."

"Does everything have to come so difficult? I would think if it's meant to be, it would be easy."

"Maybe. Maybe not." Jared shrugged. "It came easy for Jasmine and me at first, but we had our struggles after mar-riage." Jared stood up, roughly. "My point is this: Everything with value comes at a cost. Maybe that cost is later, maybe it's now; but you don't go into a burning building without a cost, and you don't enter into a Christian marriage without a little warfare." Squeezing Mike's shoulder, he continued. "So are you going to go into the building or stay out on the side-walk, where it's safe?"

Jared walked away, leaving Mike to ponder and wrestle the thoughts. Grace felt worth every ounce of the trouble, but what if Lyle wanted back into her life? He'd just seen her that day of the zoo trip for the first time in seven years. Had he remembered how beautiful her oversized eyes were? Did he remember the porcelain smoothness of her skin? And what about Grace herself? Did she still see what she saw in Lyle all those years ago?

The alarm sounded, jolting Mike into action. He suited up, running for position in the truck. His comrades joined him, and they were all in place within seconds. The fire engine roared to life. Mike put his headset on and prepared for the code. A traffic accident, single car involved. Occupant trapped. Mike's stomach lurched.

Arriving at the scene, the vehicle rested on its roof, its hood wrinkled into an accordion and a woman outside what had been the driver's door. Her foot appeared lodged under the car. The men jumped out, and Mike went straight for the Jaws of Life. It looked like their old friend would get one last usage before retirement.

Jared assessed the situation. "Her foot is trapped beneath the brake pedal." The two men exchanged a glance, and they set the jaws to lift the vehicle from the woman. She was conscious but too numb to say anything. Even to scream. Mike whispered to her while he worked, hoping to keep her as calm as she appeared.

In less than a minute, they had the vehicle lifted, and the real work began. Firefighters covered the victim with a blanket to protect her and donned safety glasses. "This is going to be very loud. Stay calm, and we'll have you out in a moment, but this sound is frightening. I know you've been through a lot, but we have to do this." Kyle continued to calm the woman while Mike and Jared prepared for the cutter.

The cutters were necessary to release her still-trapped foot, but the minute the machinery started, she shook violently, becoming aware of her situation. The cutter sounded like a chain saw, metal teeth running down a chalkboard—a grating, eerie sound that would never leave Mike, even if he never heard it again. The cutters sawed through the brake shaft quickly, and Jared gently pulled the woman's foot from the car.

A round of applause went up as they freed the woman. EMTs were standing by and placed the woman on a stretcher. Mike looked at her for the first time. She was petite and blond, and he thought about all the people who probably loved her. What would they say when they found out her life was saved by a simple piece of machinery? The ambulance doors closed, and she was whisked away to the nearest trauma room.

Jared stood beside Mike, shaking his head. The tangled metal before them brought a somber moment of thanksgiving. CHP officers scribbled notes and took measurements. The freeway had slowed to a single lane, and angry drivers lost a little of their rage when they saw the vehicle, a mass of twisted steel.

"The CHP says her car flipped six times." John said.

"I can't believe she's still with us." Jared shook his head again. "What a miracle."

Mike headed for the engine, climbing into his seat. Jared took his own.

"You got the shopping list?" Mike asked.

"You're not going to talk about that?"

"About what?"

"The accident."

"What do you want me to say?" Mike shrugged. They witnessed accidents like that at least once a day. This was the city, after all. What was Jared looking for? "Do you think I'm crazy, like Kyle did? I need more time off?"

"I want you to think about the price you paid today. Was it worth it to get the jaws for her?"

"What?" Mike's head spun in a thousand directions. "Of course it was worth it. What is up with you?"

"What if today was your last day with us? What if someone decided to avoid the roadblocks and barreled down the freeway while you tried to save that woman? How would you spend today if it was your last?" Jared was always such an intense friend, and for once, Mike didn't appreciate it. He felt trapped, as though he needed a set of Jaws of Life for himself.

He searched his mind for the answer, knowing full well Grace and Josh were the only people who came to his mind. They were his first thought every morning, his first prayer request each day. "She's worth the cost. Is that what you want to hear? I fell in love with her about the time I saw her marching into the principal's office with her blond hair flipping in her righteous anger for Josh." Mike smiled, looking down at his clasped hands. "What good will it do me?"

"The woman in that car could have been Grace. Are you going to take a chance and make a fool of yourself or let her slip away without knowing if she was worth fighting for?"

"I haven't decided yet."

Jared gave an exasperated snort. "So if you throw her into the arms of another wealthy Los Altos tycoon, will you feel the least bit responsible?"

"She won't agree to a simple dinner alone with me. These last few weeks, we've been inseparable, and yet, she's afraid to be alone with me. What would I do to her?"

"Love her. Give her something she wants but she's afraid of."

"What are you, Dr. Laura, all of a sudden?"

Jared pulled off his goggles, leaving a rim of grime around the edges. "Mike, I've known you a long time, and I have never seen a woman occupy so much of your mind or your time. Go get her! I'll have no respect for you until you do."

Mike gulped. Jared made it sound so easy, but would it be?

fifteen

Grace dressed Josh in his Sunday suit, complete with a tie. She buttoned his top button and cinched the tie. "Now, go brush your teeth. Grandpa will be so proud."

"Mom, why do we have to dress up for Grandpa? Isn't he nice?"

"He's very nice, but you've never met him. I want to make sure you look your best for your first impression." Grace brushed back Josh's bangs.

"How come he's coming today?"

"Mommy made a mistake a long time ago, and I haven't talked to your grandpa in a long time. I was wrong, and God didn't like all that silence. Tonight I get to tell your grandpa I'm sorry."

"Do I have a grandma?"

Grace bristled at the question. It was so much easier when Josh just cooed and accepted everything with a gummy smile. "Yes, you have a grandma, but she's not coming today."

"Why?"

"We'll ask Grandpa, okay? Maybe she wanted to wait to meet you. To hear all about you first."

"Or maybe she's still mad at you." Josh scampered off for his toothbrush, and Grace flopped on the sofa. She broke into laughter, wondering who raised this child.

The doorbell rang, and Grace froze. She felt her heart rise and fall with all the violence of a gun battle within her. She drew in several deep breaths, but nothing calmed her.

She finally ran to the door and opened it roughly.

Her father appeared shorter, with more lines in his face—not the smile lines she remembered, but sagging, etched lines that drew his whole expression downward. His eyes were still the clear gray-blue she'd inherited, and they glistened behind his tears.

"Dad!" Grace crumbled into the outstretched arms of her father and held on as tightly as she could without hurting him. She finally pulled away, her newly made-up face now a streaky mess. She could taste the salt-laden make-up on her tongue.

"Gracie, how beautiful you've grown."

"I think I've just grown old, Dad." Grace laughed. "I feel that way."

He bowed his head, shaking it. "No, no, Darling. You glow like a light. You must be very happy here."

"Josh has made me very happy, Dad. I can't wait for you to meet him." Grace shook her downcast head. "I can't believe I've been so stubborn and denied you of each other."

"We were all stubborn, bullheaded, and ridiculous, but that's in our past. Where is the boy?" Her father walked in slowly, and Grace noticed how his back was slightly stooped.

"Dad, are you okay?"

"Oh, all those years of hammering nails have just taken their toll on this old back. That's all."

"Sit down, Dad. I'll get Josh." Grace could see Josh peeking around the doorway, his brown eyes wide and curious. She placed her hand on his cheek. "You ready?"

Josh nodded. Grace's father had settled into the sofa, tapping his foot nervously. Grace took Josh by the shoulders and led him around to the front of the couch. Her father's mouth dangled and his arms were outstretched.

"Joshua Blake Brawlins," George Brawlins croaked out the

name. "You look just like your uncle." He squeezed his grandson into a tight embrace, while Josh crinkled his face, clearly enduring the show of emotion. "Doesn't he look like Georgie, Grace?" He asked, referring to Grace's brother.

"I guess he does, Dad." Grace smoothed some lint off the back of the sofa. "So, Dad, Mom didn't come with you?"

"No, Gracie, your mother hasn't been well."

Grace felt her breathing increase. She took shallow, jagged breaths. "What do you mean, not well?"

"She's just tired all the time and doesn't leave the house much." George looked back at his grandson. "But your grandmother sent something for you. Let me go get it."

Grace watched her father leave for his car with Joshua closely on his trail, and she knew her mother had done no such thing. Harriet Brawlins would never find it in her heart to give Grace's illegitimate son a gift. It went against everything the woman stood for.

George reentered with an enormous plastic bag from Toys 'R Us. The receipt floated onto the floor, and Grace picked it up. The receipt was from the local toy store, and Grace knew her father had once again tried to protect her from Mother's wrath.

"Dad, what is all that? Did you buy out the toy store?"

"I haven't had a grandson for six years. I have a lot of buying to do."

Grace put her arm around her father, "No, Dad. You being here is all the gift we needed."

The doorbell rang, and Grace froze. "Who could that be?" Thoughts of Lyle drifted into her head. Would he ruin her reunion with her father?

George and Josh were frantically opening boxes and discarding paper about the room. The two of them hadn't even heard the door. Grace answered it, and Mike's towering frame filled the doorway.

"Mike." She sighed with relief. "It's you. I thought you had to work until morning."

"I traded, against my chief's wishes, but it was important I come."

"I have my father here tonight."

Mike looked around her, and offered a wave to her father, but George was blissfully tearing open packages with Josh. "It looks like I have a run for my affections." Mike looked down upon her, his blue eyes nearly melting her with their intensity.

Grace wanted to fall into his arms, to tell him no one could ever compete for her affections, but she squared her shoulders, holding steady. "Joshua will always love you, Mike, no matter who comes into his life."

"It wasn't Josh I was speaking of."

She swallowed audibly. "Mike, please don't play with my heart. I don't think I could bear it."

He cupped her cheek into his hands. "May lightning strike me if I should ever play with your affections, Grace. Joshua may have brought us together, but look at these last months, Grace. Are they really only about Josh? Or is there more between us?"

"Who's this, Grace? Bring your friend in." George interrupted them, and Grace forced herself to breathe, to come back into the moment. Her father was there, and she could hardly maintain her joy at having the only three men she ever loved in her home at the same time. It was too good to be true, and somehow Grace feared it would crumble around her feet.

"Grandpa! This is Fireman Mike."

George stood. "Ah, so this explains why the radio controlled fire engine was such a hit."

"Dad!" Grace looked at the pile of boxes that now towered above Josh. "What did you do in that store?"

George laughed, standing to shake Mike's hand. "This is my only grandchild. Your brother may never settle down. I have a right to spoil Josh—isn't that right Fireman Mike?"

"Absolutely, Sir." The two men shook. "Grace has been counting the days until your arrival. I'm glad you came, Mr. Brawlins."

Grace's father brushed her cheek. "Me too. Don't know what took me so long. This is my princess. She never walked anywhere. Danced everywhere she went. What a joy she's been." George looked as though he might cry again, and he coughed away the emotion. "I'm just a silly old man now, but she's still a princess."

"I agree." Mike said, and Grace felt warm.

She fanned herself a bit. "Does anyone want iced tea?"

❧

"Grandpa, Mom said Grandma was waiting to meet me." Josh looked up with his huge brown eyes, looking for the approval Grace always wanted from her mother, but never seemed to get. "Do you think she'll like me?"

Grace's anger flooded, and she could feel her face heat. She wouldn't have Josh search for something he'd never find in the coldhearted mother who abandoned Grace at her time of need.

George sat back down, patting his knee. To Grace's surprise Josh readily went. She laughed to herself. Nothing like a bag of toys to gain a child's confidence. Grace only hoped George wouldn't be the once-a-year Santa and disappear.

"Grace, I'll help you get the tea." Mike took her hand, leading her into the kitchen. Grace's feet felt molded to the floor.

She was so anxious to hear her father's answer. Was George Brawlins still answering for his wife who couldn't forgive their wayward daughter?

"Grace!" Mike's insistence finally caught her attention.

She followed him to the kitchen. Searching his face, she looked for something physically wrong with him, something that might tell her it was okay if he abandoned their family. She couldn't depend on a man for happiness, and she didn't. *The Lord is my shepherd. The Lord is my shepherd*, she reminded herself.

Mike turned, and she faced those sapphire eyes again. They would be her undoing. She braced herself against the countertop, letting him fumble through her kitchen for glasses and ice.

"Your father seems thrilled to be here."

"Uh-huh," Grace answered absently.

"What about you? Are you happy to see him?" Mike broke apart the ice in the trays.

Grace smiled. "He's still the same father I grew up with— the one who spoiled me rotten and loved me, no matter what."

"Grace, you have to forgive your mother."

Grace felt ashen as the blood flowed from her face. She met Mike's eyes in a challenge, "Oh, no, I really don't."

"Grace, every day I am reminded how we only get one chance at this life. We can waste it being angry and bitter, or we can move on. You need to move on. If your mother chooses to lose out on Josh in her life, that's her loss, but you can't let her control you any longer."

"She'll hide behind her religion for a lifetime. She'll be too happy to tell me of my sins and where I've gone wrong. I don't need that in my life."

"Maybe not, but you don't need this resentment either. This harms you, not her. She's done enough damage to herself. You don't have to punish her, Grace."

"Why would you care?"

Mike set the ice tray down and came toward her. She felt her heart pound under his gaze. "Because I love you, Grace. Or haven't you noticed?"

She shook her head. "No. No, you don't. You love Josh." She pushed him away at his chest, but he wouldn't be turned away. He enveloped her in a hug.

She felt his heart hammering as he pulled her against his chest, and she could barely breathe in her emotions. He whispered at her ear. "I watch people die nearly every day, Grace. I don't say things I don't mean, and I don't feel there's time to waste in this lifetime." He knelt down to one knee, holding her hands in his. "Grace Brawlins, I love you. Say you'll marry me and make me the happiest man on earth. I'll be a good father to Josh. I'll love him as my own, and the Lord willing, we'll give him siblings."

Grace pulled her hand away, clutching her heaving chest. She tried to keep her wits, to tell herself this was really happening, but it was too unbelievable. "We haven't even been on a date."

"Grace, we've been together constantly for months. What do you mean we haven't had a date?"

"Alone. We haven't even been alone. What if Josh goes to his friend's house, and you find I'm not the woman you thought. What if—"

"Grace." He stood up, cupping her face into his large, masculine hands. "In every emergency since I met you, my mind is constantly reminded of you and Josh. I have more reason than ever to get home safely."

"Well, we do care, Mike."

"I could waste another year dating you because that's

probably more appropriate by all accounts, but I don't want to waste that time, Grace. I don't want Josh to go any longer without a father, and more importantly, I don't want to go any longer without you."

Grace felt her whole frame shivering. This was too much for her. Her father spoke in the other room; the man she loved professed his love for her. When would the dream end? When would she wake to find none of this had really happened?

"I've been on my own so long. I don't know how to trust someone. I don't know how to live with someone else."

"We'll learn together." He reached into his windbreaker, pulling out a black velvet box. He bent to one knee again, opening the box. Inside twinkled a modest, brilliant-cut diamond, surrounded by tiny Ceylon sapphires—the color of Mike's eyes. She breathed deeply, first focusing on the ring then on the love in Mike's expression. She looked around her, noticing the ice beside them was melting on the counter, and she reached for a piece, its chill telling her this was truly unfolding.

"Mike," she said breathlessly.

"Grace, will you do me the honor of becoming my wife and allowing me to adopt Joshua as my own?"

Grace tried to process the words over the sound of her pounding heart. "I haven't even kissed you." Grace shrugged. "What if there's no passion for us?" She suddenly giggled. She felt her heart race every time he looked at her. Was she even strong enough to withstand his kiss?

And with that, he stood, pressing his lips against hers. She melted into him, feeling passion to her toes. Her hair even tingled at the roots. He kept kissing her, and she returned it with a zealous desire, unlike anything she'd ever felt. She looked at the ring and relived his romantic notion of more children.

There would be no ugly check, only the unrelenting joy she had felt forbidden to feel with Joshua.

"Well?" He asked again.

"Oh, Mike, really? You're sure about this?"

"I've never been more certain of anything in my life. Of course, I planned to ask you all romantically at our fancy dinner out, but I couldn't wait. Looking at you tonight, I just couldn't wait. You are beautiful, Grace, and I want to be with you as soon as possible."

Grace let her head fall back, relishing the love she felt for this man, unable to comprehend that he loved her in return. She closed her eyes, wanting to remember everything about this moment. She felt her hair tickle her back, and she flinched as Mike placed a soft kiss on her exposed neck. Looking up at him, she met his lips again before pulling away.

"Yes, I'll marry you. I'd marry you tomorrow, if I could."

"Shh." He placed his forefinger at his lips. "Don't give me any ideas. You, my dear lady, are going to have a church wedding. We are going to declare our love and commitment before the entire congregation. Joshua is going to give you away, and I am going to accept you with bells on."

Grace started to giggle, covering her mouth. "I can't believe Josh got his prayer answered."

"His prayer?"

"When we first met, and you told him about Jesus, he started praying for you to be his father. I told him how ridiculous the idea was, but—"

"But Josh knew God was bigger than what the two of us had in store."

"How will you explain to your friends that you're marrying a single mother? Will they hate me?"

"I work in a firehouse, Grace. My friends have seen so much tragedy, so much pain. . .they know when you find love, you reach out and grasp it with all your strength."

"Even if it's with someone who carries her sin on her sleeve."

"You've been forgiven, Grace. It's time you forgave yourself, or you are only the reincarnation of your mother. I was reading my Bible, and I found the perfect verse for you. I memorized it."

"Am I ready to hear this?"

"This is Jesus speaking about the sinful woman, 'You did not give me a kiss, but this woman, from the time I entered, has not stopped kissing my feet. You did not put oil on my head, but she has poured perfume on my feet. Therefore, I tell you, her many sins have been forgiven—for she loved much. But he who has been forgiven little loves little.' " Mike brushed her cheek with the back of his hand. "The only difference between your sin and someone else's is that yours is obvious because of Josh. Forgive yourself, Grace, and your mother, because she loves little."

Grace felt the tears glide down her cheeks. "I love you, Michael Kingston."

Suddenly, a piercing shriek invaded their happy moment. "It's my beeper." He grasped it, reading the message. "There's a fire, and the men need back-up. I have to run."

"But Mike—"

"Wait to tell Josh, please. I want to be there when he finds out he gained a father and a grandfather in the same day."

"I love you," she called after him.

He came beside her, lifting her lips to his own. "I love you too. Enjoy the time with your father, and make the most of it."

"I will, I promise."

Mike dashed through the living room. "Good-bye Mr. Brawlins. A pleasure to meet you, Sir. I have to run. Josh, take care of your mom, Bud. I'll be back soon."

Grace held the sparkling diamond in her hand, closing the box and placing it in her pocket. It didn't feel right to put it on before they had officially sealed the deal.

With the roar of the truck, he was gone, leaving Grace somewhere between euphoria and overwhelming loss.

sixteen

Mike scratched his head, trying to figure out what happened. First, he went to support Grace with her father. To encourage her to forgive. Somehow, he'd spoiled his proposal and given her the ring in a clumsy, unromantic fashion—in her kitchen, no less. What woman wanted to be romanced in the kitchen?

He slapped his forehead. "And you wonder why you're still single." He said to his reflection in the rearview mirror. He could hear the whirl of the sirens in the distance. He knew this fire must be at least three alarms by the sheer number of engines on the case. His heart began to race, and thoughts of Grace soon disappeared behind the cloud of smoke in front of him.

Six ladder trucks surrounded an old hotel on Main Street. Adrenaline flowed freely now, and Mike ran to an engine and suited up. Jared waited for him. "I'm glad you made it. We're on together."

"Great. Anyone in the building?"

"We don't know," he said while running alongside Mike. "Someone over at the convenience store reported a woman went in a couple hours ago, but he doesn't know if she came out."

Mike looked up, flames licked the sky from the roof, and the crash of windows could be heard blowing out. The constant roar of ladder trucks and crews surrounding the building was deafening. At least one hundred and twenty firefighters were in place, raining down a solid wall of water over the structure.

The captain looked at Jared and then to Mike. "Engine 6, you two are on tonight. We got report of a woman living on the second floor. I need you in there."

Mike instinctively looked up. The sun was beginning to diminish behind the mountain, and he knew darkness would envelop them within the building. The combination of smoke and darkness could be deadly. His heart began to pound with anticipation. To get in and out, with their occupant and all of them alive, that was his mission.

"Let's go!" Jared yelled in compliance, and the two of them, connected by radio and wearing oxygen tanks and special goggles, were off.

Mike muttered a prayer to himself. He waited for a team to ax through the door, and they stood back while heat and billowing smoke stormed at them. Then, along with Jared, he burst into the building.

"She's on the second floor, central." Captain Jackson said into the radio. "Engine 19 is on the infrared camera. You've got heavy smoke straight ahead. Veer right. The seat of the fire is on level three, at your left."

The eerie sound of his own breathing echoed in his mask. Their path had filled with dark, looming smoke, and Mike began to worry for the unknown woman on the second floor. So far, they hadn't seen any flames except for those lapping through the rooftop, but the smoke was thick and dark. Without goggles, Mike and Jared would have been completely blinded. Without a mask, probably confused and disoriented, possibly unconscious. He feared for the woman and knew their quest was growing more important by the second.

❧

Grace could hear the wail of several fire engines, and she grew more fearful with each passing truck. Josh and his grandfather had opted out of dinner at a restaurant and were happily barbecuing hamburgers in the yard.

Josh scrambled in, "Mom, there's a lot of smoke coming from that fire. Is Fireman Mike okay? Can we call him?"

"There are a lot of firefighters out there. Mike is probably drinking a soda on the engine." Grace scrubbed the countertop with extra effort, trying to hide the terror she felt inside. Was this how life would be, married to a man who put his life on the line? Grace didn't know if her weak heart could stand it.

"Grace, I told Josh to come on inside. The smoke is awfully thick out here. Between me scorching these burgers and the fire, I don't know which is worse."

"Thanks, Dad."

"Mom, the fire isn't going to burn our house, is it?"

"No, Josh. The engines would be a lot closer if we were in any trouble. I'm sure whatever is going on, Mike has it under control."

"No fire is tougher than Mike, Mom. He's been in burning buildings and rescued people lots of times. That's why he's such a hero." Josh leaned with his elbows against the counter, trying to appear as cool as possible. "None of those other dads at school can say that."

"That's right, Josh. Mike is certainly a hero." Grace forced back her tears. Dicing vegetables for the salad, she hummed to herself, drowning the sound of sirens and running engines from her mind.

Her father came behind her, hamburgers in hand. Placing the dish on the counter, he placed his arm around her. "Your friend will be just fine, Grace."

"How did you know?" She faced him. George Brawlins knew things about her she never had to admit. Life with him had always been that way. "How did we let things come between us, Dad?"

He shook his head. "We had such high hopes for you, Gracie. We planned you'd be high-powered lawyer or executive of some type. We never understood that God had something better for you."

Grace sniffed. "I can see where my being a single mother wouldn't be your idea of success." She watched Josh scamper to the radio-controlled fire engine, and the noise soon took away the opportunity for him to overhear. "It's hard, Dad. I'm so exhausted when I come home from work, yet there's dinner to be made or groceries to be bought, homework, dishes, baths, then after a few hours sleep, I get up and start all over again." She noticed her father's pained expression. "Oh, Dad, I'm not complaining. I'm just saying I know from the outside it must seem like a stupid thing to try and raise him alone. But his father didn't want him born, and I just felt like the only one who could truly protect him."

"It was your choice, Gracie. Your mother and I had no right to interfere. We should have helped you, not abandoned you. We were wrong." He bowed his head. "So wrong."

"I'm going to marry Mike, Dad."

"Your mother will come around. Maybe she'll come to the wedding."

"I'm going to call and invite her, Dad. I will eventually forgive her, and I hope she'll do the same." Another siren blasted past the house, and Grace slammed the knife to the counter. "Another one!"

"Mom, come here! The fire's on TV!" Josh sat on top of his new engine, watching the news. Huge flames burst from the top of a quaint, downtown hotel built at the turn of the century.

Grace searched the firefighters in the background, looking for Mike's jacket, praying to see "Kingston" scrawled across a yellow back. The newscaster came on, dressed in a jacket and tie.

"We're here at Main Street in downtown Los Altos. As you can see there's a raging fire within this building that was currently empty while renovations took place." The camera angle zoomed in for a shot of the hot orange flames. "It is our understanding that firefighters are inside searching for a lone woman who is believed to be on the second floor."

"Oh, please, don't let it be Mike." Grace bit her lip nervously.

The newscaster shoved a microphone in a firefighter's face while he talked into a radio. Brusquely, the camera equipment was shoved away. "I'm working here. You mind?"

"I've got to get down there. Dad, can you watch Josh?"

"Gracie, it's illegal to go to a fire. There's nothing you can do."

"I can pray, Dad. I'll stay far away, I promise. I just want to see that he's out of the building." Grace grabbed her keys and shot through the door. She waited for her car to turn over, urging it several times, and raced to the scene. Police officers stood at the corner, turning people away. Grace ripped the engagement ring from her pocket, placing it on her left finger. She admired it for only a second, before parking the car haphazardly.

"Turn around, Miss." The police officer halted her with his palm. "No spectators."

"My fiancé is a firefighter. I just want to stand here and pray. I won't pass. I promise."

He scanned her warily. Then her sparkling ring captured his attention. "It's unusual, but as long as you stay right here,

I got nothing against it."

Some of the flames had ceased since she'd watched the television, and she thanked God for that. Still, she didn't know where Mike was. Why did she assume he was in the building? There were hundreds of firefighters on the scene. Surely, it wasn't him. Yet she prayed with all her might. Sinking to the roadside grass, she knelt, beseeching the Lord to deliver Mike back to her. She'd barely had a chance to tell Mike she loved him. Sure, she'd agreed to marry him, but did he know it was for him alone? Not for Josh to have a daddy?

Minutes seemed like hours, and it was then that she noticed the camera crew. Rushing across the street, but not past the protective line, she called out to the reporters.

"Hey there!" She raised a hand. "Are the firefighters out of the building?"

The reporter shook his head. "Not that we know of, but the chief hasn't got time for us, and they have no one on for media, so I couldn't tell you for sure. You know somebody in there?"

A helicopter hovered over them, and Grace had to scream her answer. "One of the firefighters just asked me to marry him tonight, then he got called away to respond to this fire."

The cameraman looked to the reporter, and Grace felt the pair drop something around her neck. Looking down, she saw it was a press badge. "Wait a minute, I can't go in there. I promised the officer."

"The fire's nearly under control, Miss, and this makes a much better story."

Grace watched a woman carried from the building into an ambulance. The firefighter removed his mask, and Grace nearly fainted with joy. "Mike!" She ran toward him, and he wrapped her into a hug.

"Grace, what are you doing here?" He looked up at the

building, and seeing the flames were under control, he removed his gloves too. "The chief will have my head. I'm already in hot water." He embraced her. "Oh, who cares?" He kissed her quickly.

"I'm leaving. I don't want you in any trouble. I just wanted you to know that I love you, Mike! I've loved you for the longest time, and you're right. I don't want to wait anymore. Every day that passes is too long. We'll tell Josh today!"

He twirled her off her feet, covering her face in kisses. Then he stopped and lifted his helmet. "I'm getting married!"

A group of fireman hollered, and before Grace knew it, an important-looking man approached them. She stood tall, blinking rapidly, both from the smoke and her fear.

"Grace, this is Fire Chief Radson." Mike stood at attention. "Chief, this beautiful woman has just agreed to be my wife."

"Well, I'll be." The fire chief crossed his arms, clearly intent on letting them enjoy the moment.

A microphone jammed in her face, and she realized with embarrassment that their whole love scene had been caught on tape. *Film at 11*, she thought.

"Is it true, you just came from that burning building, and this woman accepted your proposal?"

"Actually—" Mike began to clarify when the reporter cut him off. Clearly, their version was a better story.

"And is it true, Miss, that you broke through a police barricade to profess your love to this hero?"

Grace giggled relentlessly, unable to control her emotions. "Yes, it is true. And I'd do it again for the love of this man. He's worth every river I might forge."

Mike kissed her again. "Hey, is that thing on?" He asked the cameraman who nodded. "Joshua, you tell God a great big thank you tonight. I'm going to get to be your daddy." Mike thrust a fist toward the sky. "Our prayers were answered, little guy!"

Grace kissed him again, snuggling against his smoky scent. "You are my hero."

"And you're mine, Grace."

They embraced and shared a passionate kiss. Grace flickered her ring finger for the camera.

A Letter To Our Readers

Dear Reader:

In order that we might better contribute to your reading enjoyment, we would appreciate your taking a few minutes to respond to the following questions. We welcome your comments and read each form and letter we receive. When completed, please return to the following:

Rebecca Germany, Fiction Editor
Heartsong Presents
PO Box 719
Uhrichsville, Ohio 44683

1. Did you enjoy reading *Grace in Action* by Kristin Billerbeck?
   ❑ Very much! I would like to see more books
      by this author!
   ❑ Moderately. I would have enjoyed it more if

   _____

   _____

   _____

2. Are you a member of **Heartsong Presents**? Yes ❑ No ❑
   If no, where did you purchase this book?_____

   _____

3. How would you rate, on a scale from 1 (poor) to 5 (superior), the cover design?_____

4. On a scale from 1 (poor) to 10 (superior), please rate the following elements.

   _____ Heroine   _____ Plot

   _____ Hero   _____ Inspirational theme

   _____ Setting   _____ Secondary characters

5. These characters were special because_____

_____

_____

6. How has this book inspired your life?_____

_____

_____

7. What settings would you like to see covered in future **Heartsong Presents** books?_____

_____

_____

8. What are some inspirational themes you would like to see treated in future books?_____

_____

_____

9. Would you be interested in reading other **Heartsong Presents** titles?   Yes ❑   No ❑

10. Please check your age range:
    ❑ Under 18   ❑ 18-24   ❑ 25-34
    ❑ 35-45   ❑ 46-55   ❑ Over 55

Name _____

Occupation _____

Address _____

City _____ State _____ Zip _____

Email _____

Ozarks

*F*our young women learn that there is no hiding from God—and love—in small towns among the rugged bluffs and clear-water lakes of Arkansas and Missouri. Amity and Emily face the biggest transitions of their lives, while Andrea and Carla fight the change that threatens their comfortable existence. Each of the four is about to embark on a journey of trust.

The road to contentment may be long and winding, like an Ozark highway. What does God have in store for each woman along the way?

paperback, 464 pages, 5 ³⁄₁₆" x 8"

❤ ❤ ❤ ❤ ❤ ❤ ❤ ❤ ❤ ❤ ❤ ❤ ❤ ❤ ❤ ❤ ❤

Please send me _____ copies of *Ozarks*. I am enclosing $5.97 for each.
(Please add $2.00 to cover postage and handling per order. OH add 6% tax.)

Send check or money order, no cash or C.O.D.s please.

Name_____

Address _____

City, State, Zip _____

To place a credit card order, call 1-800-847-8270.
Send to: Heartsong Presents Reader Service, PO Box 721, Uhrichsville, OH 44683

❤ ❤ ❤ ❤ ❤ ❤ ❤ ❤ ❤ ❤ ❤ ❤ ❤ ❤ ❤ ❤ ❤

···Heart♥ng···

Any 12 Heartsong Presents titles for only $27.00*

CONTEMPORARY ROMANCE IS CHEAPER BY THE DOZEN!

Buy any assortment of twelve *Heartsong Presents* titles and save 25% off of the already discounted price of $2.95 each!

*plus $2.00 shipping and handling per order and sales tax where applicable.

HEARTSONG PRESENTS *TITLES AVAILABLE NOW:*

_HP58 FREE TO LOVE, D. English	_HP238 ANNIE'S SONG, A. Boeshaar
_HP137 DISTANT LOVE, A. Bell	_HP242 FAR ABOVE RUBIES, B. Melby
_HP177 NEPALI NOON, S. Hayden	and C. Wienke
_HP178 EAGLES FOR ANNA, C. Runyon	_HP245 CROSSROADS, T. Peterson
_HP181 RETREAT TO LOVE, N. Rue	and J. Peterson
_HP182 A WING AND A PRAYER,	_HP246 BRIANNA'S PARDON, G. Clover
T. Peterson	_HP254 THE REFUGE, R. Simons
_HP186 WINGS LIKE EAGLES, T. Peterson	_HP261 RACE OF LOVE, M. Panagiotopoulos
_HP189 A KINDLED SPARK, C. Reece	_HP262 HEAVEN'S CHILD, G. Fields
_HP193 COMPASSIONATE LOVE, A. Bell	_HP265 HEARTH OF FIRE, C. L. Reece
_HP194 WAIT FOR THE MORNING,	_HP266 WHAT LOVE REMEMBERS,
K. Baez	M. G. Chapman
_HP197 EAGLE PILOT, J. Stengl	_HP269 WALKING THE DOG, G. Sattler
_HP201 A WHOLE NEW WORLD,	_HP270 PROMISE ME FOREVER, A. Boeshaar
Y. Lehman	_HP273 SUMMER PLACE, P. Darty
_HP205 A QUESTION OF BALANCE,	_HP274 THE HEALING PROMISE, H. Alexander
V. B. Jones	_HP277 ONCE MORE WITH FEELING,
_HP206 POLITICALLY CORRECT,	B. Bancroft
K. Cornelius	_HP278 ELIZABETH'S CHOICE, L. Lyle
_HP209 SOFT BEATS MY HEART,	_HP282 THE WEDDING WISH, L. Lough
A. Carter	_HP289 THE PERFECT WIFE, G. Fields
_HP210 THE FRUIT OF HER HANDS,	_HP297 A THOUSAND HILLS, R. McCollum
J. Orcutt	_HP298 A SENSE OF BELONGING, T. Fowler
_HP213 PICTURE OF LOVE, T. H. Murray	_HP302 SEASONS, G. G. Martin
_HP214 TOMORROW'S RAINBOW,	_HP305 CALL OF THE MOUNTAIN, Y. Lehman
V. Wiggins	_HP306 PIANO LESSONS, G. Sattler
_HP217 ODYSSEY OF LOVE,	_HP310 THE RELUCTANT BRIDE, H. Spears
M. Panagiotopoulos	_HP317 LOVE REMEMBERED, A. Bell
_HP218 HAWAIIAN HEARTBEAT,	_HP318 BORN FOR THIS LOVE, B. Bancroft
Y. Lehman	_HP321 FORTRESS OF LOVE, M. Panagiotopoulos
_HP221 THIEF OF MY HEART, C. Bach	_HP322 COUNTRY CHARM, D. Mills
_HP222 FINALLY, LOVE, J. Stengl	_HP325 GONE CAMPING, G. Sattler
_HP225 A ROSE IS A ROSE, R. R. Jones	_HP326 A TENDER MELODY, B. L. Etchison
_HP226 WINGS OF THE DAWN,	_HP329 MEET MY SISTER, TESS,
T. Peterson	K. Billerbeck
_HP233 FAITH CAME LATE, F. Chrisman	_HP330 DREAMING OF CASTLES, G. G. Martin
_HP234 GLOWING EMBERS, C. L. Reece	_HP337 OZARK SUNRISE, H. Alexander
_HP237 THE NEIGHBOR, D. W. Smith	_HP338 SOMEWHERE A RAINBOW,
	Y. Lehman

(If ordering from this page, please remember to include it with the order form.)

·······Presents·······

__HP341 IT ONLY TAKES A SPARK, *P. K. Tracy*
__HP342 THE HAVEN OF REST, *A. Boeshaar*
__HP346 DOUBLE TAKE, *T. Fowler*
__HP349 WILD TIGER WIND, *G. Buck*
__HP350 RACE FOR THE ROSES, *L. Snelling*
__HP353 ICE CASTLE, *J. Livingston*
__HP354 FINDING COURTNEY, *B. L. Etchison*
__HP357 WHITER THAN SNOW, *Y. Lehman*
__HP358 AT ARM'S LENGTH, *G. Sattler*
__HP361 THE NAME GAME, *M. G. Chapman*
__HP362 STACY'S WEDDING, *A. Ford*
__HP365 STILL WATERS, *G. Fields*
__HP366 TO GALILEE WITH LOVE, *E. M. Berger*
__HP370 TWIN VICTORIES, *C. M. Hake*
__HP373 CATCH OF A LIFETIME, *Y. Lehman*
__HP377 COME HOME TO MY HEART, *J. A. Grote*
__HP378 THE LANDLORD TAKES A BRIDE, *K. Billerbeck*
__HP381 SOUTHERN SYMPATHIES, *A. Boeshaar*
__HP382 THE BRIDE WORE BOOTS, *J. Livingston*
__HP390 LOVE ABOUNDS, *A. Bell*
__HP394 EQUESTRIAN CHARM, *D. Mills*
__HP401 CASTLE IN THE CLOUDS, *A. Boeshaar*
__HP402 SECRET BALLOT, *Y. Lehman*
__HP405 THE WIFE DEGREE, *A. Ford*
__HP406 ALMOST TWINS, *G. Sattler*
__HP409 A LIVING SOUL, *H. Alexander*

__HP410 THE COLOR OF LOVE, *D. Mills*
__HP413 REMNANAT OF VICTORY, *J. Odell*
__HP414 THE SEA BECKONS, *B. L. Etchison*
__HP417 FROM RUSSIA WITH LOVE, *C. Coble*
__HP418 YESTERYEAR, *G. Brandt*
__HP421 LOOKING FOR A MIRACLE, *W. E. Brunstetter*
__HP422 CONDO MANIA, *M. G. Chapman*
__HP425 MUSTERING COURAGE, *L. A. Coleman*
__HP426 TO THE EXTREME, *T. Davis*
__HP429 LOVE AHOY, *C. Coble*
__HP430 GOOD THINGS COME, *J. A. Ryan*
__HP433 A FEW FLOWERS, *G. Sattler*
__HP434 FAMILY CIRCLE, *J. L. Barton*
__HP437 NORTHERN EXPOSURE, *J. Livingston*
__HP438 OUT IN THE REAL WORLD, *K. Paul*
__HP441 CASSIDY'S CHARM, *D. Mills*
__HP442 VISION OF HOPE, *M. H. Flinkman*
__HP445 MCMILLIAN'S MATCHMAKERS, *G. Sattler*
__HP446 ANGELS TO WATCH OVER ME, *P. Griffin*
__HP449 AN OSTRICH A DAY, *N. J. Farrier*
__HP450 LOVE IN PURSUIT, *D. Mills*
__HP453 THE ELUSIVE MR. PERFECT, *T. H. Murray*
__HP454 GRACE IN ACTION, *K. Billerbeck*

Great Inspirational Romance at a Great Price!

Heartsong Presents books are inspirational romances in contemporary and historical settings, designed to give you an enjoyable, spirit-lifting reading experience. You can choose wonderfully written titles from some of today's best authors like Hannah Alexander, Irene B. Brand, Yvonne Lehman, Tracie Peterson, and many others.

When ordering quantities less than twelve, above titles are $2.95 each.
Not all titles may be available at time of order.

SEND TO: **Heartsong Presents** Reader's Service
P.O. Box 721, Uhrichsville, Ohio 44683

Please send me the items checked above. I am enclosing $_____
(please add $2.00 to cover postage per order. OH add 6.25% tax. NJ add 6%.). Send check or money order, no cash or C.O.D.s, please.
To place a credit card order, call 1-800-847-8270.

NAME _____

ADDRESS _____

CITY/STATE_____ ZIP _____

HPS 11-01

Hearts♥ng Presents
Love Stories Are Rated G!

That's for godly, gratifying, and of course, great! If you love a thrilling love story but don't appreciate the sordidness of some popular paperback romances, **Heartsong Presents** is for you. In fact, **Heartsong Presents** is the *only inspirational romance book club* featuring love stories where Christian faith is the primary ingredient in a marriage relationship.

Sign up today to receive your first set of four never-before-published Christian romances. Send no money now; you will receive a bill with the first shipment. You may cancel at any time without obligation, and if you aren't completely satisfied with any selection, you may return the books for an immediate refund!

Imagine...four new romances every four weeks—two historical, two contemporary—with men and women like you who long to meet the one God has chosen as the love of their lives...all for the low price of $9.97 postpaid.

To join, simply complete the coupon below and mail to the address provided. **Heartsong Presents** romances are rated G for another reason: They'll arrive *Godspeed!*

YES! Sign me up for Heartsong!

NEW MEMBERSHIPS WILL BE SHIPPED IMMEDIATELY!
Send no money now. We'll bill you only $9.97 post-paid with your first shipment of four books. Or for faster action, call toll free 1-800-847-8270.

NAME _____

ADDRESS _____

CITY _____ STATE _____ ZIP _____

MAIL TO: HEARTSONG PRESENTS, PO Box 721, Uhrichsville, Ohio 44683

YES10-96